"Did it ever occur to you that I just don't like you?"

Jan wasn't prepared for Clark's chuckle and the ready smile that almost made her forget her low opinion of him. "Not really," he admitted, drawing out the words. "I think you're simply trying to hide the deep attraction you have for me."

"That's the most preposterous—"

"Not at all. B.J. isn't reason enough for the way you've responded to me. I've been around enough women to..."

"I'm quite sure you've been around plenty of women, but don't throw me in with the masses." Her composure was slowly returning. "At the risk of being repetitive, let me say I don't like you. Furthermore, I don't respect you. And I'm afraid those are only two of the many ingredients required for me to be attracted to a man."

"You don't know me—yet—and what you're afraid of is the romantic tension between us that's crackling like static during a thunderstorm...."

Dear Reader,

The people, places and descriptions in this story come strictly from our imaginations. However, there is a real Valentine, Texas, and each February romantics from all over the world send their cards to this West Texas post office to be remailed with its special Valentine station LOVE stamp.

Kate Denton

Kate Denton is a pseudonym for the Texas writing team of Carolyn Hake and Jeanie Lambright. Friends as well as coauthors, they concur for the most part on politics and good Mexican restaurants, but disagree about men—tall versus short—and what constitutes good weather—sun versus showers. One thing they definitely agree on is the importance of romance.

Books by Kate Denton

HARLEQUIN ROMANCE

2870—WINNER TAKES ALL
2966—A BUSINESS ARRANGEMENT
3057—HOME SAFE
3123—FIRM COMMITMENT
3223—TO LOVE AND PROTECT
3281—NO OBJECTIONS
3332—CROSS PURPOSES

Valentine, Texas

Kate Denton

Harlequin Books

TORONTO • NEW YORK • LONDON
AMSTERDAM • PARIS • SYDNEY • HAMBURG
STOCKHOLM • ATHENS • TOKYO • MILAN
MADRID • WARSAW • BUDAPEST • AUCKLAND

To Jim.
For reasons too numerous to list, but you know them all.

ISBN 0-373-03398-2

VALENTINE, TEXAS

First North American Publication 1996.

This edition published by arrangement with Harlequin Books S.A.

Printed in U.S.A.

CHAPTER ONE

BOXES overflowing with mail crammed the back room of the rural post office in stacks so high they threatened to topple at any second. Jan Armstrong glanced around and grimaced. From the looks of things, she was making no progress—the stacks seemed taller now than when she'd started.

It was her first experience with the post office, much less with this special seasonal workload. February meant valentines. Here in Valentine, Texas, it meant cards arriving from all over the world to be imprinted with the town's unique heart-shaped postmark before dispatch to final destinations.

To Jan the sight was depressing—cards of all sizes, their envelopes a variety of colors from basic white and sophisticated cream to raucous shades of red and pink. She couldn't help but pity the senders of these love notes. *Darn fool romantics*. There must be zillions of card-writing sentimentalists out there. *Everyone but me*, she thought ruefully. For her, the upcoming lovers' holiday held as much appeal as Christmas did for Scrooge.

Yet little more than a year ago, she'd been a romantic, too. Back then, she'd had a job she loved...a husband she loved.... *If only*... Her reveries were interrupted by the ping of the counter bell signaling a waiting customer.

"Anybody home?" a voice called out.

"Down here," she said, gazing up from her cross-legged position on the floor as the face of a man appeared over the counter—actually the ledge of a Dutch-style door.

Casually he leaned on the countertop, a half-filled bottle of Coca-Cola gripped in one hand. "Well, hello there. How about a game of post office, pretty lady?"

Jan forced a smile at the lame joke. She'd heard it more than once from local cowhands, especially those from the Montgomery place who made a ritual of teasing her. "May I help you?" she asked, the words husky, difficult to get out now that she'd gotten a better view of the visitor. The man might not earn points for originality, but as far as looks went, he unquestionably rated a ten. Jan suspected there were plenty of female postal workers who would eagerly dispense kisses to him, game or no game.

She hadn't seen a male this handsome since leaving Los Angeles...in fact, she'd seen few men this handsome in L.A. itself—his regular features framed by a strong jaw, vivid blue eyes, and an easy smile revealing nice white teeth. One tooth was slightly crooked, an endearing flaw which warded off physical perfection. As their eyes met, he grinned confidently, his expression suggesting that he was sensing her approval. Jan stood up, self-consciously dusting the backside of her jeans.

Her customer straightened, also, bringing the Coke to his lips and taking a long swallow as he downed the rest of the bottle. He set it on the counter. "I need a book of stamps," he said, pulling out his wallet and placing a ten in her hand.

Jan gave him the stamps, then opened the cash register for change, all the time aware of his unyielding gaze. He was staring almost to the point of rudeness. Yet she was determined not to shy away, her hazel eyes assessing him in precisely the same unflinching manner.

He was long and lean and dressed in well-worn jeans and a Western-styled shirt. A brown leather belt with a silver buckle circled his trim waist and she didn't have to see his feet to know he wore boots. No denim jacket or sheepskin coat, so popular in these parts, however. Instead he sported an expensive leather bomber jacket.

Aside from his jacket and his spectacular good looks, the man typified a male Valentine resident. He could be a local ranch hand with that deep tan and slight squint, acquired around here from working out of doors, not from lazy days lounging on a sunny beach. But he wasn't someone she recalled meeting before, even though the face and those crayon-blue eyes were vaguely familiar.

Jan watched as he lay the cola bottle sideways on the counter and with a flick of his wrist sent it spinning. When the motion finally stopped, the bottle was pointing her way. He glanced at the bottle, then at her. Although he said nothing more about silly kissing games, an insolent smile tugged at his lips, a smile that Jan found more annoying by the minute.

"Is there anything else I can get for you today?" She tried to stifle the indignation which was creeping into her tone. Whoever this guy was, she didn't like him. He was too handsome, too sure of himself, cocky enough to believe she would actually entertain the notion of playing "Post Office" or "Spin the Bottle"—or whatever—with him. Little did he know. She'd rebuffed plenty of rural Romeos since arriving in Valentine and she could rebuff him, too. Just let him try something.

But he didn't. "I guess that about covers it for now," he said, walking across the anteroom to drop the bottle in a wastebasket, then turning around to face her. "Maybe another time." He grinned again and headed out the door, leaving Jan with her mouth agape. The words might have been innocuous, but the expression suggested more. *Arrogant male!*

She checked the wall clock, then slammed the top half of the wooden door shut. It was four minutes past twelve and the post office was officially closed. Thank goodness.

Jan slumped into the handiest chair and sighed, disgusted with the stranger for subjecting her to this meaningless encounter and at herself for becoming irritated. Also troubling her was the flickering desire that had stirred within her. "What's wrong with me?" she asked woefully, as one who prided herself on being unaffected by handsome, flirty males. Even when the attention did occasionally rattle her, it was caused more by aggravation at the presumptuousness of the situation, than by a reaction to the man's supposed charms.

Yet now...now she hardly knew how to explain her feelings. It was as though she'd experienced some kind of ridiculous attraction to this person, the idea of him actually holding her and kissing her strangely appealing. She shook her head in strenuous protest, willing the emotion away. She didn't want to respond to him, to any man for that matter. Her heart was just starting to mend and she had no desire to jeopardize the healing process.

For another thirty minutes she worked feverishly at postmarking valentines, but found the task increasingly depressing and decided to quit. Three weeks remained until Valentine's Day. The mail could wait. "My heart's just not in this now," she told herself, then grimaced at the unintended pun.

After locking up, she headed out the front door and across the street to Neumann's Grocery. Her Aunt Sally was ill and Jan wanted to buy ingredients for chicken soup. Hot soup would be just the thing for a sore throat.

Sally MacGuire, or Sally Mac as she was called by almost everyone, was the town's postmistress, and also the reason Jan had spent her Saturday morning at the post office. Jan was by training a teacher, but she was only too happy to fill in for the woman who'd taken her in, who'd comforted her, who'd helped her realize that life goes on. And chicken soup was another service she could bestow, a small payback on the massive personal debt she owed.

"No good deed goes unpunished." The adage came to mind the second Jan entered the market and saw that, regrettably, *he* was there. Leaning against the magazine rack near the door, backlit by the big red neon heart that always shone in Neumann's storefront window, her recent customer appeared to be engrossed in conversation with a group of locals. But upon seeing her enter, he excused himself and came over to her. "So, we meet again. Must be Kismet."

"Or maybe just my bad luck," she retorted.

"Possibly, if you want to be a cynic," he said, extending a hand. "I'm Cla—"

"And I'm in a hurry," Jan interrupted, ignoring the hand and rushing to gather items for the soup.

But as she threaded her way through the narrow, makeshift aisles, he stayed with her. "Are you always this unfriendly—or are you making an exception for me?"

You're definitely an exception, she wanted to answer, but held her tongue. After all, he hadn't behaved much differently from a dozen local cowhands who'd come on to her. Why he managed to be such a bigger annoyance than the others was beyond her comprehension. Still, this being a free country and she being off duty meant she didn't have to talk to him if she didn't want to. And she didn't want to. Responding to him right now would serve no purpose—probably just encourage him to keep pestering her.

He didn't pursue her further, but patiently stood nearby, scanning a *Newsweek* magazine while she checked out her items and scribbled her signature on a receipt. In accordance with small town practices, the grocer would bill her at the end of the month.

As Jan reached for the bag, though, her hands connected with his.

"I'll take this," he announced in a commanding voice, folding the *Newsweek* into a back pocket and tucking the groceries in the crook of his arm.

Jan shrugged in resignation. Short of creating a minor scene, there was no way of retrieving that bag from his grasp. Discretion was the only route for her to take in this situation. Valentine was a community where gossip flowed faster than rainwater through a dry creek bed and Neumann's was a conduit for that gossip, dispensing more rumors than food.

Once they were on the sidewalk and out of earshot, she grabbed for the bag. "I'm perfectly capable of carrying my own groceries," she snapped.

He deftly pulled the bag out of her reach and eyed her carefully before shaking his head. "I'm not so sure. You don't look all that strong to me. In fact, the next blue norther'll probably blow you clear off your feet."

Jan knew she was too thin at the moment, just a little over a hundred pounds and, at five-four, the crown of her chestnut-brown hair barely reaching his shoulder. Looks were deceiving, however, and she could take care of herself. Too bad this pompous stranger didn't comprehend that fact.

She'd seen his type many times over in Los Angeles, the type who fancies himself as God's gift to women. In fact, the West Coast or New York was where he belonged, not here. A second glance in his direction told her that he seemed a step out of place in Valentine, his russet hair professionally styled, and the fit of his shirt suspiciously custom tailored. Plus he had a worldliness that reminded her of Glen. Ah, that was the rub! *Glen*. Suddenly Jan found justification for her behavior. No wonder she'd overreacted to the man—the last thing she needed in her life was a reminder of her ex-husband.

They crossed the street to her Mitsubishi and he opened the door, setting the bag on the passenger seat. "Thanks," she said grudgingly.

"My pleasure, ma'am." He touched his head in a mock salute, before assisting her into the car. "See you around."

Jan watched in her rearview mirror as he trotted back toward the grocery store and disappeared inside. "Not if I see you first," she vowed.

Only a few blocks lay between the post office and Sally MacGuire's modest frame home, yet Jan would pass by most of Valentine's sights on her way. The small town was similar to many in central Texas with its long, single main street flanked on each side by stores and a smattering of offices. For eleven months a year its appearance closely matched that of its sister towns.

But in mid-January those similarities abruptly ended when the last Christmas bows and wreaths were put away and overnight the community exploded with a hodgepodge of valentine arrangements. Lamp posts, signal lights, shops, trees, anything that didn't move got decorated. As well as a few things that did, such as the sheriff's patrol car which now had big red see-through hearts covering the shields on its front doors. The observance lasted for a month and then the town went back to normal—for the most part.

Within minutes Jan was home, entering the back door and placing the groceries on the kitchen table. Then she sought out Sally's room where her aunt sat propped up in bed, a romance novel in hand. Sally smiled, acknowledging her niece's presence, and eased off her reading glasses, allowing them to dangle on a cord around her neck. "Hello, dear. How are things with the mail?"

"The mail's fine," Jan answered hastily. No use distressing her aunt by revealing the accumulation of cards taking place. As postmistress Sally took her duties very seriously and only something as debilitating as the flu could keep her away from them, especially now.

Sally was a romantic, a never-married woman of indeterminate age who still believed in candy, flowers, honeyed messages and all the other trappings of the Valentine's Day observance. Perhaps it was living in a town with a billboard announcing: "Welcome to Valentine, Texas. We take our name to heart." Or maybe it was the weighty influence of the February mail crush, but for a few weeks each year Sally seemed to get her role of postmistress confused with that of Cupid. She prided herself on having personally fostered at least a dozen long-lasting marriages.

"I can put in some extra hours next week if you need me," Jan said. Sally operated on a tight schedule and she probably needed reassurance that her illness had not thrown her off. But Jan didn't anticipate problems. In a few days, there would be several part-time helpers coming in to get the greetings on their way. "Right now, though," she announced, "I'm going to fix chicken soup for dinner."

"That sounds wonderful. You're really spoiling me. Jan..." Her aunt paused a moment. "I do love having you here."

"And I love being here. There's nowhere I'd rather be." Jan patted the older woman's leg affectionately. "I'd better get busy. There's a bird waiting for me in the kitchen."

Nowhere I'd rather be. Jan pondered the words as she mechanically went through the process of cooking. It was a surprising revelation considering how miserable she'd been when she arrived in Valentine last fall. Until then, Jan had only visited a few times, and most of those trips were so long ago that she hardly remembered them.

Her father and his sister were total opposites. One a government emissary, a globe-trotter who'd taken his family to posts all over the world. The other a nester who still lived in the old family house where the two siblings had grown up. Like Sally, Jan was developing a sense of contentment in Valentine, almost as though she belonged here.

Would anything happen to spoil that contentment? Jan hoped not. She could stand the month-long holiday aggravation, and most of the other negatives were insignificant. The biggest problem was being unmarried, which made her a target for more male attention than she wanted, such as having to deal with the likes of her morning visitor. With any luck, however, he was merely passing through. After all, she'd been in town for months and hadn't seen him before. Feeling calmer, she reached for the pepper mill to season the soup.

The next morning, Jan went alone to the small white church for worship services, Sally not yet well enough to accompany her. Walking down the aisle and searching for an unfilled pew, she halted dead in her tracks. There *he* sat, the pesky stranger, right beside the Montgomerys—Garrett and his grandson B.J. Was this a coincidence or was he staking out all the places she went?

Get a grip on yourself, she chided. *This is a church and he has as much right to be here as you do.* Rights or not, Jan couldn't see herself enduring an hour with him in close proximity, so she eased into a pew near the back.

She had difficulty keeping her mind on the hymns and the sermon. Her eyes kept straying to the nape of the newcomer's neck, to the red-brown hair brushing the collar of his white shirt, to the strong profile displayed whenever he turned his face to the side. Once he even glanced back her way, catching her in the act of watching him and giving her a cynical crooking of an eyebrow to tell her so. From then on, she kept her gaze fixed on the pulpit.

Her concentration didn't improve though. The man was intruding on her life, even going so far as to interfere with her Sunday worship. Her list of grievances continued to grow until it reached the point where Jan realized she was overreacting again. She forced her thoughts onto the Montgomerys.

B.J. was her pupil. The sweet-faced seven-year-old had filled part of the recent void in her life. And Garrett—Garrett was extra special. A widower with no family except his grandson, the rugged rancher had become almost a father figure to Jan during the past few months—just as Sally had become a surrogate mother. Although Jan had hardly known Garrett before moving in with her aunt, she'd quickly developed a deep respect and liking for him.

Garrett was big—a good six-four—with a weathered sixty-year-old countenance more fitted to Mount Rushmore than to a mere mortal, and a personality as strong as Texas white limestone. Behind this rocklike image, however, beat the heart of a gentle and compassionate man.

He'd stepped right in when she'd arrived in Valentine, encouraging her to frequent his ranch, the Lazy M, teaching her to ride a horse, letting her talk out her problems.

Even after personal tragedy struck him a fierce blow, Garrett had remained sensitive to her needs. His only child, a daughter, Toni, was killed in a car accident shortly after Jan arrived in Texas. As a result, his grandson B.J. went to live at the Montgomery ranch and Garrett had offered Jan a position tutoring, telling her how much it would help the little boy. The local school provided a quality education, but the child required individual attention, he'd said. "B.J. needs you." Garrett had never added, "And you need him," even though Jan knew it to be true. She'd been working at the Lazy M over a month now and had not once regretted the decision.

Restoring her career was one of the hundreds of ways in which Garrett had been an unrelenting supporter. Together, he and Sally had given Jan the courage to put one foot in front of the other, to try and make the most of her life. She owed him a great deal.

As the congregation rose for the last hymn, "Rock of Ages," Jan realized that, thanks to her random musings, she'd missed most of the service. This had to stop. Despite a strong desire to escape out the door the moment the song ended, she couldn't let some good-for-nothing cowboy continue to ruffle her hind feathers, as Sally would say. So Jan sighed, took a deep breath, then calmly slipped out of the pew, making herself chat with acquaintances, pausing to shake hands with the pastor and waiting on the front steps for Garrett and B.J.

It wasn't just a coincidence, Jan decided, that her nemesis had been sitting next to the Montgomerys, because he now accompanied them as they emerged through the arched double doors. Apparently, he either worked for Garrett or was a guest at the ranch.

B.J. hugged Jan, and Garrett kissed her on the cheek. The stranger held back, but that dratted smile still played about his lips, as though he perceived Jan's reluctance to see him and was enjoying it. And despite all her efforts at indifference, she couldn't help but remember yesterday—the momentary feelings he'd generated.

Garrett, unaware that this wasn't their first encounter, took Jan's arm as he made introductions. "Clark, Jan Armstrong, my grandson's teacher. Jan, this is B.J.'s father, Clark Brennan." There was no warmth in Garrett's manner as he spoke.

Jan fought for composure, her eyes widening with confusion as she turned her attention from the grim-faced rancher to Clark. *Of all people*! She'd had no idea. According to Garrett, B.J.'s father was a parental failure, at best an apathetic, intermittent presence in his son's life who hadn't bothered to visit the child in a year. Even Toni's death hadn't been enough to bring him back. *So why has he come now*?

"Mr. Brennan," Jan acknowledged, her voice nearly as frosty as Garrett's.

"Ms. Armstrong," he replied, the grin now missing, even though his words were cordial. "Pleased to meet you." He waited a moment, as though contemplating adding "again." Instead, he said, "My son's very fond of you." He rested a hand on B.J.'s shoulder.

"And I of him," she said crisply. Jan knew good manners called for polite conversation, but she simply couldn't stand around making idle chitchat with such a sorry excuse for a human being. "If you all will pardon me, I need to get back to Sally. Goodbye."

Before waiting for a response, Jan rushed down the church steps toward her car.

Her mind was in overdrive all the way home. The stranger was Clark Brennan, B.J.'s father. She had yet to hear a good thing about the man. Garrett regularly lambasted him for neglecting his son, the rancher's outbursts generally coming when B.J. was having a rough day. The boy, himself, rarely mentioned his father. When he did, it was only to show Jan a postcard or knickknack from some distant place. There was never any comment that indicated closeness between the two of them. As far as Jan knew Clark hadn't made so much as a phone call since B.J. lost his mother.

The best she could determine was that a divorce occurred when B.J. was a mere toddler, and from that time on Clark had had little to do with the child.

Why hadn't she been more inquisitive? As B.J.'s teacher, it behooved her to know what his father had been doing all those years. Not that it would have changed the outcome—the son would still have been ignored—but at least Jan would have had some background to guide her.

To think that she'd found Clark even remotely appealing was more disquieting than ever. Jan consoled herself with the reminder that she'd been more put off than taken in by him. Anyway, any earlier impressions had been replaced by total contempt since she'd learned his identity.

She adored children and in her short time as tutor to B.J. had already grown attached to him. Sometimes she had to rein in her feelings, realizing they went beyond what was appropriate for a teacher and pupil. But she couldn't help caring about him. And if she were a mother.... A twinge of regret pulled at Jan's heart. If she *were* a mother, she'd put the needs of her child first and her own second. "*Most* people do—including most fathers," she said aloud as she pulled into the driveway.

She sat in the car a few moments, continuing to absorb the shock. One thing was certain, she would be better prepared for her next meeting with Clark Brennan. Three off-kilter encounters were quite enough and she knew just what she was going to say on the fourth go-round. She'd tell him exactly what she thought about his treatment of his son, let him know exactly how much B.J. had suffered because of his father's indifference. Jan had no patience for irresponsibility—especially when it affected children.

She went in the back door, kicked off her black pumps in the kitchen and checked on the pot roast she'd left on the burner. It had simmered sufficiently; all she had to do was toss in some vegetables.

With lunch on its way and a cup of coffee in hand, she headed toward the glassed-in sun porch where Sally sat watching a church service from Dallas. A punch of her aunt's finger on the remote control and the sound muted. "You're home early."

"I felt like I should get back," Jan said. She hadn't mentioned Clark Brennan yesterday and she wasn't sure how to bring up the subject now. "Evelyn Sanders said to tell you 'hi,'" she said, stalling for time until she figured out how much to reveal. "You were missed."

"Well, I would hope so," Sally retorted goodnaturedly. "I've been going to that church so long, the pew should have an imprint of my bottom by now."

A knock sounded at the front door, then Garrett's voice boomed from the hall. "Sally Mac, Jan? Are you girls decent?"

"Come on back," Sally answered, as heavy footsteps on the hardwood floor announced Garrett's approach.

"I'm here to check on the patient," he said with a solicitous smile, obviously at home as he unceremoniously plopped down in a rocking chair, resting his felt Stetson on his knee.

"The patient is fine," Sally answered. "Almost well. I'll be back at work tomorrow... but where's B.J.?"

"With his daddy," Garrett blurted out, his tone leaving no doubt as to the level of his disgust. Jan wished she'd prepared her aunt.

"Clark Brennan is in Valentine?" Sally exclaimed.

"Showed up Friday acting as if he owned the place! Who does he think he is interrupting our lives now?" Garrett's voice was still a roar. "Frankly I'd just as soon he'd never come back."

"Maybe it's good that he did," Sally soothed.

"What's good about it? Sally Mac, you know as well as me that all he ever did for the boy was send support checks and too many presents. Big deal." Garrett fairly spat out the words. "We don't need his money and we don't need him hanging around spoiling the boy rotten, catering to his every whim."

Jan silently agreed that B.J. didn't need another adult catering to him. Garrett was bad enough. Only recently had she managed to convince him that overindulging B.J. wouldn't make up for the loss of his mother or the absence of his father. But gifts aside, she had to agree with Garrett—biased though his view might be—the appearance of Clark Brennan could hardly be considered good news.

Garrett stood up, walking over to the window and gazing out at the garden. Abruptly he turned toward Jan and Sally. "After six years of token fatherhood, he's decided he wants the boy." Garrett raked his fingers through his thick hair, hair the color and texture of steel wool. "Well, we'll see about that. I've got an appointment with a lawyer in Temple next week. I'm going to find a way to get Brennan out of our lives once and for all."

CHAPTER TWO

WANTING to give Garrett and Sally privacy to discuss matters further, Jan checked on lunch, then went for a walk in the backyard. It was a trek she made often, looking upon the small lawn and garden as a haven, a place to relax and clear her head.

Jan brushed a cluster of fallen leaves off a wooden picnic table bench and sat down, then glanced toward the house, toward the glassed-in porch. Garrett was gesturing wildly, ventilating at full throttle with Sally as his audience. Although the two had been close friends for years and he shared most of his feelings with her aunt, Jan had never seen him unleashing his temper like this.

She wondered what had transpired between Clark and Garrett and Toni that brought about such rancor. But she knew all too well how quickly the tides of love and fortune could turn. She was a walking example of the peccadilloes of life.

I thought I'd be married forever. Jan had voiced those feelings to Sally more than once, the reality continuing to catch her unaware. Almost two years had passed since the beginning of her ordeal, but the wounds were still painful. Even now Jan could feel the heart-stopping shock and embarrassment at Glen's arrest—the federal marshals invading the bank where he worked and taking him away in handcuffs, all captured for *Live at Five* that very night on television. "Arrests were made today in the Los Jardines Land

Development Project with charges of fraud and bribery leveled at prominent bank officials...."

At the time, she was known as "Miss Jan," a TV kindergarten teacher. She thrived on the role and had just begun to attract a loyal following when she was dismissed because of the publicity surrounding Glen. "You're too controversial...no longer a good role model for our young viewers," she'd been told.

Even though her husband had eventually won his release on a plea bargain—agreeing to testify against higher-ups in exchange for reduced charges—the emotional and financial costs had been staggering. The money part was secondary to Jan, however, when compared to the relief of Glen's being free. The two of them would simply have to start over.

She had expected difficulties as they struggled to put their marriage back on track. The fundamental element of trust—a necessary base for any marriage—had been lost. Regardless of Glen's reasons, what he'd done was wrong. But she believed strongly in the sanctity of marriage and was willing to work at repairing the damage created by her husband's ill-advised actions. Jan took it for granted that he felt the same way.

Perhaps that was why Glen's announcement was so chilling. She'd come home from a day of substitute teaching to find him packing. He was leaving California, and with it all memories of his unhappy experience. Including her. Glen wanted a divorce. "I have to go out and find myself," he informed her. "Alone." Then he'd discarded her like last year's calendar.

That was when a devastated Jan had fled to Valentine and to Sally, her favorite relative. She could have joined her parents who were now in Europe, but their frenetic life-style offered no appeal during this period of emotional upheaval. Jan knew she would be unwillingly drawn into their nonstop social world and expected to participate in their activities. She needed peace and quiet, not parties—and Valentine was about as quiet a place as one could hope for. Except when February was approaching.

A woman with a newfound prejudice against romance residing in "Loveville," U.S.A. was rather comical, she thought, shaking her head in bemusement. Thankfully, February was a short month. Pretty soon the St. Valentine's Day hoopla would fade. And, when the holiday rolled around next year, she'd have her life together once more, maybe have a job in Dallas or Austin or San Antonio. For now, she'd just continue taking one day at a time. Jan looked up to see Sally and Garrett, heads bent together, still in deep conversation.

What to do? Jan didn't want to intrude, but she didn't want them to think they'd banished her to the garden, either. She slipped in the kitchen door, switched off the oven and burners and wrote Sally a note. In her haste to come home after church, Jan had foregone her ritual of picking up a metropolitan Sunday edition on the way. She'd get one now.

The newspaper stand in front of Neumann's was empty, and Jan drove on to Annette's Diner. She was walking out the front door with a *Dallas Morning News* in hand when she almost collided with B.J. hurriedly entering the diner.

"Hi, Jan, I forgot my hat." He ran toward a corner booth in the back.

If B.J. was there, Clark couldn't be far behind, and sure enough, he was next door, gazing at items in the window of Handy Hardware, when she appeared on the sidewalk. As he looked toward her his face formed a frown. "Too bad I didn't realize you worked for Garrett," he said, moving her way. "Then your hostility yesterday would have made sense. If I had known you were under his influence, I wouldn't even have attempted being friendly."

Jan glanced around, hoping no one had overheard. Except for the two of them, the street was empty. "You have an interesting notion of 'friendly,'" she said. "And I had no idea who you were then. Maybe you'll just have to accept my so-called 'hostility' as a simple reaction to someone who was being too pushy." She brushed past him and stepped off the curb. Clark was right on her heels, but before she could warn him to stop following her, B.J. ran up.

"While you're talking, can I play Annette's video games?" he asked.

"Sure." Clark reached into his pocket for some change, but the boy rejected his offer.

"I have my *own* money," B.J. said in a tough seven-year-old voice. He started back inside, without even giving Jan his customary hug, or telling her goodbye.

"So, to what does Valentine owe the *honor* of this visit?" she asked. The tension between Clark and his son was all too palpable and Jan wanted to lash out at him on B.J.'s behalf. Father and son might be spending time together, but it was clear her young charge was unhappy.

"Aren't most visitors to town treated with a bit more cordiality and hospitality?" he responded, ignoring her question. "You'd never make it as a representative from the welcoming committee. At least Garrett gave me a place to sleep."

"Probably so he could keep an eye on you," Jan retorted. Garrett might be mad at Clark, but he was crafty, sly as an old fox. While Clark was with B.J., Garrett would want him close at hand—and Jan didn't blame Garrett for being cautious or suspicious. "What I can't understand," she said, "is why he allows you to be here at all."

"It's not a matter of Garrett's *allowing* anything. I have every legal right to be with my son."

"Legal right! What about moral rights?"

"What's so moral about keeping a man from his child? Chew on that awhile, Ms. Armstrong," Clark barked as he turned on his heel and disappeared into the diner.

Jan climbed back in her car feeling bewildered and somehow in the wrong. No matter how hard she tried, she couldn't push the feeling aside. So much for being better prepared. Now it was Clark Four, Jan Zero. Her grand plan to give him an earful about his treatment of B.J. had blown up in her face. It was a mistake losing her temper and letting Clark get the upper hand. Jan vowed to be calmer in their future meetings. She had to be or she'd never get her message across about the way he'd slighted his son.

"Would you believe it—B.J.'s father turning up unexpectedly like this? I think it's been close to a year and a half since he was last here." Sally stabbed at an elusive carrot cube with her fork. She and Jan were seated at the kitchen table, Garrett having turned down an invitation to share Sunday lunch with them.

"When did he arrive?" Jan asked. "There was no mention of him when I was tutoring B.J. on Friday."

"According to Garrett, he took everyone by surprise. Just showed up on the front step about dark that night. Garrett's in a regular snit about it."

"With good reason," Jan said.

"Maybe."

"There's no 'maybe' about it. Garrett has every reason to be furious with Clark. When I think of his cavalier behavior toward B.J., I just want to—" Jan stopped herself, remembering that Sally was still ill. She'd had enough stress today dealing with Garrett. There was no point in Jan dumping on her aunt, too.

"Perhaps there were extenuating circumstances." Sally chewed the carrot reflectively. "I think Garrett should cut Clark a bit of slack."

"You're too willing to give everybody the benefit of a doubt, Aunt Sally. Garrett should boot him out of town and you know it." Sally was the kindest person Jan had ever met and she envied her aunt's patient unending tolerance of people. In this instance though, it was absolutely undeserved. "I can't understand why Garrett's being so civil to him. The man is reprehensible."

"Don't rush to condemn him, Jan. Remember that old Indian saying, 'Never judge a man till you've walked a mile in his moccasins.' He hustled to Texas the minute he learned about Toni's death."

"Minute?" Jan rolled her eyes to the ceiling. "It's been over two months. Where has he been, for Pete's sake?"

"Any and everywhere. Where *hasn't* he been? Surely you've seen some of his work on television?"

Jan shook her head. "Not that I recall."

"Well, I knew you didn't watch much...can't say as I blame you after all you went through...but I didn't realize how far removed you were."

"Seeing your husband publicly humiliated is enough to make anyone switch off the set, and leave it off. So what exactly does Clark Brennan do?"

"He's a newscaster, a foreign reporter for one of the networks...I can't recollect which one, but he's become quite well known in the past year or so. His broadcasts from the Middle East and Africa have gotten him all sorts of awards." Sally paused for a sip of iced tea. "And his coverage during that civil war last winter was nothing short of heroic. The man obviously has nerves of steel. During one telecast there were bombs almost bursting over his head."

"Now that's a rather appealing image," Jan said wryly. "I wouldn't mind bursting a bomb over his head myself—if only to rattle his cage a bit."

Sally studied her niece. "Why are you so resentful toward a man you met just this morning?"

"Actually it wasn't our first meeting. He came in the post office yesterday." There was no need in telling Sally about those other encounters. Jan still felt bruised.

"Then the Brennan ladies' man reputation is obviously overrated," Sally replied. "According to the ratings polls, he has the highest female viewing audience of any reporter, yet you seem to have come away totally unimpressed."

"That's putting it mildly. I suspect that any ladies' man stories were generated by him. He's got a very high opinion of himself. Let me tell you, he's arrogant and...and—"

"Since when is arrogance a crime?"

Jan thought she saw Sally trying to suppress a smile. "With him it ought to be," she answered defensively. "But that's irrelevant anyway, now that I've heard about him and his son." She pushed her plate back. "What did he have to do, finish an assignment before he could be bothered with minor matters like his own motherless child?"

"It's not as bad as it sounds. Clark told Garrett that he was trapped in a remote area for an extended period. He telephoned as soon as he was able. But during those months, there was simply no way he could get out or even contact B.J."

"Spare me. There's always a way—when there's a will. Surely Garrett didn't fall for that tall tale."

"Listen to you, child, carrying on so. Do you want to hear the rest of this or not?" Without waiting for Jan to answer, Sally continued. "Clark called again as soon as he got back to New York. Garrett admitted that he saw no reason to tell him about Toni's car accident—and he figured B.J. wouldn't mention it, either, not the way he is these days—so withdrawn. It seems that Clark just happened to learn the news when he chanced upon a friend of Toni's in a restaurant. Needless to say, he was a mite upset about Garrett's omission. He apparently left for Valentine within hours."

"Well that still doesn't explain all those other years. And it sounds like a lame excuse to me. He 'just happened to hear...' Give me a break."

"Is that the reason you're so willing to take sides against him? Or could there be something else at work here? Maybe something on the order of you protesting too much." Sally tilted her head and studied her niece.

"I have no idea what you're talking about," Jan said, knowing exactly where her aunt was headed and not liking it. "Let's have some more tea." She got up to refill their glasses.

Sally had been pressuring her about men almost from the second she'd set foot in Valentine—first there was Garrett's head wrangler, then a widower who owned a spread west of town, the local basketball coach, even a guy she'd heard was about to be divorced. Surely her aunt wasn't about to add Clark Brennan to her list of prospects.

No, Jan decided, Sally wouldn't risk damaging her friendship with Garrett merely to promote a romance between Jan and his erstwhile son-in-law. She sat back down and spread her napkin across her lap. "Let's just forget Mr. Brennan for now and enjoy our lunch." She held up the platter. "Are you ready for more pot roast?" But despite her attempt to table the subject, Jan knew she wouldn't easily forget him, or her aunt's probing questions.

Now Jan understood why he didn't quite fit the Valentine image. She might have been slow to guess his roots, but she'd never imagined them to be in television. The fact he'd looked familiar didn't equate to his being a TV personality. Just a face she'd forgotten. And no matter how impressed Sally might be, or think Jan was, Jan didn't care one whit about his kudos or his citations for bravery.

As a life form, he'd slipped another rung from the lower-than-low position she'd assigned him since learning he was B.J.'s father. In her book, reporters had less social value than wharf rats, especially when it came to their disregard for the welfare of humanity. And she ought to know, having been one of the "humanity'' mistreated by the profession. Sally had called her resentful. *Who wouldn't be, in her place*? Jan had been relentlessly harassed during the problems with Glen, some of the harassers her peers, a couple even former friends.

This latest bit of information banished any resolve to confront Clark about his abandonment of his son. Instead, she planned to keep as far away from him as possible.

''So much for avoiding the guy,'' Jan grumbled as she passed through the rounded arches of Garrett Montgomery's Lazy M Ranch and up the paved driveway the next morning. The first person she spotted was Clark himself, casually straddling the corral fence as he watched one of the cowboys trying to calm a bucking horse.

The places in front of the house were taken, so Jan parked near the end of the drive, alongside a row of ranch vehicles. She climbed out, then slammed the car door harder than she'd intended, attracting everyone's attention, including Clark's, in the process. A couple of friendly wolf whistles along with several exaggerated ''Hellos!'' emanated from the group as she started down the long brick walkway toward the ranch house. Most of the attention waned as the cowhands went back to their business. But not Clark's. She sensed his eyes following her, a quick turn of the head confirming her suspicions.

For moments she remained captive to his gaze, no more comfortable with it now than she'd been before. She knew she looked good this morning, dressed in knee-high boots, a print prairie skirt, and an oversize sweater in a flattering shade of lavender. But she hadn't switched from her usual wardrobe of jeans and sweat top to entice Clark Brennan. The clothing was for B.J. She always dressed like this for his classes—an attempt to separate Jan the tutor from Jan the friend.

What was the man gawking at anyway? She might be well put together this morning, but, darn it, she was a schoolteacher, not a candidate for the female lead in a *Dallas* or *Dynasty* remake.

With that in mind, the sensuous tinglings caused by Clark's appraisals made absolutely no sense. She might be attractive, but she wasn't a knockout. So why was Clark staring like a sailor who'd been deprived of shore leave for six months?

Darn. She'd forgotten her coat and had to retrace her steps to the car. The sky was overcast and the temperature was dropping, so she'd probably need it later. One never knew in Texas. The temperature had been in the balmy seventies most of last week and just yesterday the rosebushes and Japanese maple tree in Sally's yard had indicated imminent budding. But the weather in these parts often played tricks on the unsuspecting flora, tempting them into blooming, and just when the flowers burst forth, sending in an onslaught of seasonal lows. Now, for example, with a hard freeze predicted for tonight. The thought was depressing to her. She needed the warmth of spring, not the destructive jolt of a belated winter.

When she started up the drive again, she saw that Clark had climbed down from the fence and was sauntering her way. Jan walked faster, hoping to avoid him, but he managed to intercept her halfway to the front porch.

"Sally Mac tells me you're in television," Jan started in before Clark had a chance to speak. "I'm afraid I didn't recognize you earlier. Big star though you are."

"It's quite clear you're not a fan," he replied, his tone and expression both pointedly sardonic. "So you didn't know who I was."

Jan wasn't sure whether he was referring to his occupation or his role as parent. "Other than a pain in the kazoo, I had no idea," she volleyed, concluding that he was probably a lot more concerned about his professional image than his personal one. "You're not exactly a household name." She picked up her pace, but Clark's long-legged stride easily kept up with her. "Sorry to wound your ego," she continued, hoping all the while that she had.

"Sorry? I don't think so. Seems to me as though you take perverse pleasure in doing just that."

She started to respond, to deny his accusation, but Clark stopped her, raising his hands in a gesture of defeat. "Look. I didn't walk over here to spar with you. I only wanted to ask that instead of letting hearsay paint me as a villain, we declare a truce until you get to know me better." He smiled, and it was nothing short of flirtatious, the kind of practiced smile that had undoubtedly garnered him those high marks with women viewers. But not with her.

"I think I know you as well as I need to."

"On the contrary. I deserve an impartial hearing, an opportunity for us to get acquainted before you permanently label me the dregs of society. Who knows, you might even decide you like me."

Fat chance of that, Jan thought, but if she wanted to help B.J., she had to tolerate his father—at least

for the time being. The adversarial relationship between Clark and Garrett would be enough for him to contend with without his teacher entering the fray.
"Okay, if you insist," she reluctantly agreed.

"Truce, then." He extended his hand for a shake.

This time Jan responded by accepting the offered hand, in a forced effort at politeness. But as far as knowing Clark Brennan, the less contact, the better. Especially physical contact, she decided, realizing that even the businesslike handshake made her uncomfortable.

"I'd better attend to your son," she said, starting up the steps and hoping she could put aside her wayward thoughts and hide her awkward feelings.

"He mentions you a lot," Clark told her. "I appreciate your helping him."

Jan shrugged. "It's my job." Was it her imagination or had his tone become slightly more deferential? If so, why? Did his version of a truce include winning her over as his ally instead of Garrett's? No way. She had no interest in siding with Clark.

"Not that he talks to me much just yet," Clark continued, his voice startling her in mid-thought. "But when he does, your name pops up. I'm glad you've been able to get through to him so fast." He jammed the ends of his fingers into the pockets of his jeans. "Maybe you'll share some ideas with me. Lord knows, I haven't been a smashing success so far. Of course his grandfather's influence could be partly to blame for that."

"You're being unfair. Garrett wouldn't try to turn B.J. against you, no matter how much he might want to. It sounds to me as though you're seeking someone else to blame for your own neglect." She reached for the door handle.

"So much for a truce. I see Montgomery's thoroughly poisoned your mind about me."

"Then you see it wrong."

He shook his head ruefully, as though to discount her words. "I don't think so. On the other hand, I discovered that you live with your aunt. If Garrett isn't the venomous one, then perhaps she is. From everything I hear, she and Garrett are close—real close."

"I'm glad the Valentine grapevine is in good working order, but you'd better quit trying to read between the lines. Regardless of her relationship with Garrett, and his attitude toward you, Sally MacGuire would never say a harsh word about anyone—even you."

"Then all this negative stuff came from my former father-in-law?"

"Did it ever occur to you that I'm not relying on anyone else's say-so, that I just don't like you?"

Jan wasn't prepared for Clark's chuckle and the ready smile that almost made her forget her low opinion of him. "Not really," he admitted, drawing out the words. "I think you're simply trying to hide the deep attraction you have for me."

CHAPTER THREE

"THAT'S the most preposterous—" Jan was too stunned by his brash allegation to respond as forcefully as she knew she should.

"Not at all. B.J. isn't reason enough for the way you've responded to me. I've been around enough women to—"

"I'm quite sure you've been around plenty of women, but don't throw me in with the masses. I'm not one of your giddy female fans." Her composure was slowly returning. "At the risk of being repetitive, let me say I don't like you. Furthermore, I don't respect you. And I'm afraid those are only two of the many ingredients required for me to be attracted to a man."

"You don't know me—yet—and what you're afraid of is the romantic tension between us that's crackling like static during a thunderstorm."

This had gone on long enough. His assumptions were beginning to sound as off base as Sally's. And it seemed that no matter how determined she was to hold her ground, Clark managed to disconcert her in some way. She pointedly checked her watch. "If you'll excuse me... I'm already late for a session with your son. By the way, where is he?"

"Getting dressed. I tried to help but he insisted on doing it alone," Clark said resignedly.

Jan looked up at him. There seemed to be a quiet sorrow in his voice and his eyes were so brooding, so serious, that for a second she felt sorry for him. Then she caught herself, remembering that not only had he been goading her mercilessly during the past few minutes, but that this was a man who'd selfishly ignored his child to go glory-seeking around the globe. How dare he think he could sashay back into B.J.'s life at will and expect a friendly welcome—from anyone. Sally said he had nerves of steel. Well, Sally should have added brass to that compound. Jan wasn't about to fall for any "poor me" routine.

"And Garrett? Where's he?"

"Out checking some stock."

"Thank you." She turned to go inside.

"Jan!" Just as her hand reached for the knob, the door swung open, B.J. and the smell of freshly baked cinnamon rolls enveloping her at the same time. The young boy hugged her tightly, pointedly ignoring Clark who'd followed behind.

Jan ruffled B.J.'s hair, and as she did, was unable to keep from comparing the boy and the man. Now that she knew about the relationship, there was no denying the marked resemblance between them—the same deep blue eyes, the same wavy auburn hair, B.J.'s hair a slightly lighter version of Clark's. "What are you so excited about?"

"Grandpa said Calico, the stable cat, had kittens last night. Let's go see them!"

"How many kittens?" Jan hung her coat on the hallway rack.

"Five. Two girls and three boys. Come on. I want to see them." He tugged on her arm.

"Right after your lessons are finished," she countered. As sympathetic as she was to the grieving boy, Jan had to be careful not to give in to his every demand. B.J. had grown used to such deference since coming to live at the ranch, a temper tantrum erupting when anyone said "no." But Jan had convinced Garrett that his grandson needed to accept limits. Under the steady, firm guidance of the two of them, the boy had learned self-control and reduced his outbursts. Would the improvement continue now that his father was here? Or would B.J. act up to gauge the reaction of the newcomer?

Her answer came immediately as he hit the floor spread-eagled and began screaming. "I want to see the kittens! I want to see the kittens! Now!"

Clark bent down. "Cut that nonsense out, son, and listen to your teacher." The bellowing only grew louder, B.J.'s small cowboy boots working furiously against the floor. Clark continued to talk to him, in a soft, calming voice.

Jan was surprised—and inexplicably irritated—that Clark was handling the outburst in such a sensible manner. "We want to see the kittens, too," he said. B.J. stopped screaming and looked up expectantly. "*After* lessons." The screaming started again.

Clark looked up at Jan. "Shall I cart him off to his room for some time out?"

"I think I have a better idea," she whispered, determined to correctly handle B.J.'s tantrum, even if it meant she had to endure his father a few minutes longer. She set her briefcase on the floor, then announced in a loud voice to Clark, "Why don't we go have a cinnamon roll and a glass of milk while B.J. finishes his protest?"

He nodded and the two of them made their way around the corner to the large kitchen. Rue Nell, the ranch housekeeper and cook, who had set the rolls out to cool was apparently away—this was her usual morning to buy groceries Jan recalled—so the two of them had the room to themselves. The wails from the entry hall could still be heard.

Jan turned to growl at Clark. "You'll get nowhere with him if your initial impulse is to give in."

"What do you mean? I didn't give in."

"But you wanted to." She knew she was being grossly unfair, but arguing with him seemed safer than admitting he'd done well in the situation.

"That might have been more reasonable," he said bitingly. "But I didn't want to overrule you. What difference would five minutes have made though?"

"All the difference in the world. It would've reinforced his negative behavior, that's what. Don't you know anything about dealing with children?"

"I admit I haven't been around much. That's why I asked for your aid earlier."

Jan didn't immediately respond. She could tell Clark was speaking through clenched teeth. She'd provoked him. *Good*. He'd provoked her often enough. But her objective at this time was guiding B.J., not crossing swords with his father.

"Perhaps I was being too judgmental." Her tone had become conciliatory. "I suspect right now your son is dealing with frustration in the only way he knows how, and I can empathize. Who can blame the little guy for losing control occasionally? But the displays are not appropriate and none of us would be doing him a favor to encourage them."

"You're right of course. My apologies."

Jan hadn't expected contrition, even though she knew it was tongue-in-cheek. But having categorized Clark as the sort who knew everything about anything, she'd suspected nothing less than a threat of bodily harm could make him admit being wrong—especially when he had no cause to apologize.

"As you're aware, no apology is necessary," she conceded. "Maybe we can simply agree that B.J.'s done a commendable job of adjusting to his mother's death." As much as she wanted to, Jan didn't suggest that the newest change in his life—the arrival of his unfamiliar dad—had created a setback, apparently a major one.

She was spared the necessity of further conversation by the appearance of the boy in the doorway, red-eyed, but composed.

"Do you want a sweet roll?" she asked.

He shot a glance at Clark, saying nothing.

Clark stood up. "Well, I'd better get on with my paperwork and leave you two to your lessons. See you later, son."

B.J. gave no response. Instead he sidled over to join Jan at the counter, refusing to acknowledge Clark's leaving. But as soon as the footsteps began to fade, he reached for a roll.

An hour later, Jan and B.J. were perched on the window seat in their improvised classroom. She'd finally given up on reading and spelling. Her pupil was obviously too distraught and she hoped he'd be able to talk out his feelings.

The reticent child began to open up. He couldn't keep from relating exploits of Clark— "Did you know he rode an elephant once? He sent me a picture of him on it. I can ride Speckles, but anyone can ride a pony. . . some day I'm gonna ride an elephant like him."

"I want to ride an elephant, too," Jan chimed in.

B.J. giggled. "Let's do it together. Let's go to Africa. Or Egypt. Did you know my father's been to Egypt? He's seen those pyramids in the geography book."

The child's enthusiasm, however, was tempered by resentment and vulnerability. "He was always gone. He doesn't want me. I don't know why he's here."

"Maybe he thought you needed him." As angry as she was with the father, Jan had to provide comfort and reassurance to the child.

"I *used* to need him. I don't anymore. Now I just want him to go away and never come back. I hate him, hate him...." B.J. burrowed his head in the crook of Jan's arm and she gently rubbed his back, trying to soothe him.

Jan knew B.J. didn't really hate his father. At the moment, he probably didn't know what he felt. His mother had been dead such a short time and his father was a near stranger. She suspected that B.J. *wanted* to love Clark, but he also wanted to feel loved in return. Jan herself despised Clark Brennan even more for the pain he'd caused the boy. Then she looked up to find him leaning against the doorjamb, an expression of anguish on his face. She wondered how long he'd been there. Clearly long enough to overhear B.J.'s last words.

Again, she steeled herself against feelings of pity for Clark. He'd brought this on himself. One couldn't just drop out of a child's life, then drop back in when he felt like it. He'd already missed the early years; it was too late for the nurturing father routine—and if she weren't so keen on avoiding the man, she'd relish telling him so. But that was Garrett's role, not hers.

After seeing B.J. so unhappy, Jan hoped Garrett would quickly follow through with his plan to get permanent custody of his grandson, and rid them all of Clark Brennan forever. Still, even with those aggressive thoughts percolating in her brain, she couldn't erase the image of despair she'd witnessed in Clark just a few minutes earlier. Either he was a good actor or his son's distress was beginning to tell on him. *So he had a sensitive side to him after all. Who would have thought it*?

Clark was waiting outside the door when she and B.J. left the classroom. The boy paid him scant notice as he ran upstairs to grab his jacket. As promised, Jan was taking him to the stables to see the new kittens.

Once B.J. was out of hearing distance, she spoke. "Do we have unfinished business, Mr. Brennan?"

"I just thought I'd give you one more opportunity to slap my wrist, *Ms.* Armstrong." Both his words and expression were challenging. All sensitivity had vanished. The man was clearly poised for battle.

"I don't believe in physical punishment," she said in a dismissive tone and began walking in the direction of the entry hall. Not only would she not spar with him, but she wanted to avoid any discussion whatsoever.

However, Clark wasn't to be deterred. He followed her to the front door and lifted her coat off the rack. She saw his actions as automatic rather than an effort at politeness, and he simply handed her the garment instead of helping her put it on. They stood there several moments, Clark appearing to weigh his next words.

"That's not the impression I got," he eventually said. "You and Garrett both act like you'd love nothing better than tying me to a whipping post and delivering the blows yourselves."

Jan didn't know what to say. There was no doubt that Clark was furious and any comment from her would probably make him more so, especially if she voiced her thoughts. If violence *were* an acceptable alternative, she did think he merited a good smack for neglecting B.J.

Her silence appeared to irritate him further. "Garrett's attitude, I can sort of understand . . . he's feeling all kinds of pain right now and he's striking out. But you. . . . Okay, so I offended you when we met on Saturday. That still doesn't explain why we seem to be arch enemies." He leaned over her, his jaw clenching and unclenching. "Before you stoop to any more self-righteous judging, let me warn you that you're getting involved in something you don't know a damn thing about."

He was *warning* her? Now Jan was angry, too. She wanted to tell him that he was the one who should be warned— Garrett Montgomery was not a man to monkey around with. Though she wouldn't do Clark the favor of cautioning him, she couldn't let his threatening words go unanswered. "I *do* know an unhappy child when I see one. A child who feels he's no part of his father's life."

"Perhaps so." Clark backed away, momentarily breaking eye contact and staring out the front window before looking at her again. "I readily confess I made a mistake about not spending more time with my son—a mistake I'm here to rectify. My actions made sense at the time, but now they seem self-serving. It's too late to do anything about past errors, though. Just get one thing through your head." He gestured upstairs with his thumb. "That's *my* son up there. *Mine*. And you'd better remember that fact—you and Garrett and anyone else who may be plotting his future. I don't intend to lose him, despite what you all have planned." He stormed out the front door, slamming it behind him.

Jan hugged her coat to her body, chilled by his words. Did Clark really want B.J. or was he simply grandstanding? Was he playing the concerned father not because of his son, but due to a vendetta against Garrett? If only there was some way for Jan to know. Through the glass panes she watched Clark stomp across the yard and return to where the cowboys were breaking broncos. He swung one leg over the corral and sat there, apparently lost in thought.

What had set off this attack? Likely B.J.'s earlier words. Whatever his motives, Clark couldn't have enjoyed hearing his son declare that he hated him. "Hate" might be too strong a word, but the facts were that Clark Brennan didn't deserve B.J.'s love. Garrett was right to pursue custody. He'd been the constant, the main male force in his grandson's life. Considering the kind of father Clark Brennan had been up to now, Garrett would be a fool to hand the boy over to him.

Jan couldn't help worrying about B.J. It appeared he was the prize in a power struggle between two determined men, both of whom seemed hell-bent on winning. Such a contest would only harm the boy, the boy they both professed to love.

Jan hoped Clark would see this and give up the fight. The easiest solution for all concerned would be for him to fade away like he'd done so often in the past. He was probably getting bored here anyway—or soon would. There wasn't much for a hot-shot international reporter to do on a ranch. Maybe all the forced inactivity would eventually drive him to distraction and he'd leave.

"Put on your coat, Jan." B.J. was at her side, wearing his jacket and hat as instructed. She quickly slipped into the coat and they headed out the door Clark had slammed only minutes before.

The predicted winds had barely reached breeze levels and at present the temperature was rather crisp and pleasant, with the sun peeking through the cloud cover. By the time they got to the stables, B.J. had already peeled off his hat and stuffed it in his pocket. He scratched his pony Speckles on the nose, then went in search of the kittens.

Calico, a patchwork of black, gray and yellow, was curled in the corner of the last stall, her nursing babies nestled around her. B.J.'s voice was hushed as he told Jan to "Come closer."

She knelt in the soft straw, gently stroking a kitten with her fingertips and watching B.J. pick up first one, then another. The mother cat was docile and quite willing to let them fondle her babies.

"Look at this one, Jan. He looks like Batman."

Sure enough, the gray tabby had a black half mask on its face. "He really does," Jan agreed. "Is that what you're going to name him?"

"Yeah." B.J. held the kitten up. "He's Batman. Now what about this one?" He held up another baby cat.

"That one has fur like a bobcat." Clark was resting his arms on the ledge of the stall. "What about Bobby for a name?"

For a moment, B.J.'s face showed a flash of resentment, but it quickly faded. "Bobcat. Bobby. I like it." He returned the kitten to the litter and picked up another, then glanced back up at his father. "You can come in if you want to." His invitation surprised Jan and, judging from the look on his face, Clark, also.

"Thanks," he said, then entered and sat down in the straw next to them. He and B.J. played with the cats, choosing names for the others—Marigold because of her yellow markings, and Randy and Sissy, named after former school friends of B.J. Jan refrained from entering into the discussion, preferring to watch father and son. She didn't want to like anything about Clark Brennan, but she had to give him credit for how he was interacting with the child. He may have been wounded earlier, but now was willing to accept B.J.'s tentative peace offering. Yet Clark wasn't pushing too hard, an effort Jan felt certain would have widened the gulf between father and son.

After the namings, the boy raced off to visit his pony. In his absence, the small stall now seemed cramped, confining to Jan.

"He has a lot of energy," Clark said.

"Most boys do."

For a moment Clark studied her, and Jan wondered if he was going to let fly at her again. She had made the remark in innocence, yet considering their combative relationship, he might take her words as a rebuke.

"I've already admitted that I don't know a great deal about children," he said, confirming that he had indeed taken offense. "Despite what you think about me being an uncaring father, I was trying to do the right thing. My only other choice was to bounce him between his mother and me like a Ping-Pong ball every weekend."

"Oh, really? Noble sentiments, but not much of a decision, I gather, since most weekends you were seldom within five thousand miles."

"Why do I bother trying to explain? You seem to prefer sniping at me rather than listening to what I'm trying to say."

Jan glared. As angry as she was with Clark, somehow the castigation made her feel small. It wouldn't hurt to hear him out. She was no longer as naive as she had been with Glen. Just because Clark told her something didn't mean she had to take it as gospel. "Okay, talk. I'm listening."

Clark hesitated, then began. "Like B.J., my own parents were divorced. Not a friendly divorce, either, one row after another—a tug-of-war with me in the middle. With my mother and father it was like being on a quickie European tour...if it's Monday, this must be Mother's house, Friday...Dad's. I wanted to spare B.J. that kind of trauma."

For an instant Jan sensed the child in Clark—the vulnerable child, but the empathy quickly vanished. If he'd been so hurt as a youngster, then he should have doubled his efforts to protect his son from the same fate. Surely he had enough insight to realize that his seeming indifference toward B.J. would cause similar harm.

"So you stayed away just to 'spare him trauma,'" Jan said, repeating his words and making no effort to control the bite in her tone. "Very considerate."

"I appreciate your understanding attitude," he said sarcastically. "I should have known you wouldn't buy my explanation."

"It's a bit too pat, don't you think? Like one of those human interest pieces you might have put together when you were a cub reporter. I can almost see the headline now. 'Man Denies Son's Existence For Own Good.' Of course, the headline doesn't specify *whose good*." She stood up, intent on collecting B.J. and returning to the house.

Clark stood, too, and took hold of her forearm. "Listen here, you sanctimonious—" He stopped, his attention focused behind her.

B.J. was at the door of the stall, looking up at them, the troubled expression on his face indicating anxiety.

"Hello, darling," Jan said, forcing herself not to wrench Clark's hand away. "Come in. Your father and I were just... just talking."

He shuffled his feet, stirring up a cloud of straw dust. "Speckles wants outside. Can we take him riding today?" He was shyly eyeing Clark. "We can't go tomorrow because it's supposed to snow."

"That's a good idea," Clark told him. "I'll go see if your grandpa's back and let him know so he won't worry. You pick out a horse for me to ride while I'm gone."

B.J. was quiet until Clark was out of sight, then he sat down cross-legged, nervously tracing the design on his cowboy boots. The anxious look had returned to his face.

"What's the matter?" Jan knelt beside him.

"Grandpa's gonna be mad if I go riding with... with Clark. But Speckles wanted out of his stall and I thought...I thought...." As he'd done during their lesson, B.J. burrowed his face into her shoulder.

Jan stroked his hair. Poor B.J. She was certain he was correct—Garrett would be angry if the two of them went out together. But how did B.J. know about the antipathy between the men?

"What makes you think he'll be mad, honey?" Had he caught Garrett and Clark arguing just as he'd happened upon her and Clark? Or had she been mistaken about Garrett's not trying to turn B.J. against his father?

"He'll be mad because he doesn't like my...uh, dad," B.J. said. "Rue Nell told Julio she couldn't believe 'Clark Brennan was showing his face around here.' And Julio said, 'Yeah, the boss is gonna send him back where he came from.'"

Jan was livid. She would have to remind Garrett to caution his staff about "little pitchers having big ears."

"Why did my father come, Jan?"

"Probably because he thought you might want him."

"But why did he wait so long?"

"Perhaps he had a good reason for staying away. Have you asked him about it?"

"No, we don't talk very much. Except when he tells me stories about Egypt and Africa and stuff."

"Maybe you need to talk to him more."

"Do you think so?"

"Wouldn't hurt. Then you could ask him all the questions you've been wondering about." Jan hoped she wasn't making a mistake in encouraging the boy. But it did seem that he needed to hear Clark's position and know what had happened between his parents. *Could* Clark really have acted with sincere concern for the boy or was that just some fancy tale he'd woven to rationalize his behavior? Men like Clark were experts at sugar-coating the truth. She just wished she knew a way to protect B.J., but that wasn't her job, it was Garrett's. And Garrett Montgomery could take care of his own without Jan interfering.

Jan stood up and shook the straw from her skirt. "It's getting late, honey. I promised to help Aunt Sally this afternoon by cleaning the house while she's at work."

"Is she working on the valentines?"

"That's right."

"Can we make valentines tomorrow? Please?" He lifted a kitten and hugged it to his cheek.

"After lessons," she said, stroking the soft fur on the kitten's back.

"Aaah..."

"Now, B.J. We can't play hooky two days in a row. But we will make the valentines tomorrow. We'll even cut out some hearts to hang in the barn for your grandpa's party."

"Goody," he said. "But don't forget."

"I won't." How could she? Jan thought wryly. As if the doings in town and living with Sally weren't enough, almost daily someone mentioned the Lazy M's annual Valentine barn dance. Garrett didn't do a lot of entertaining anymore. A barbecue every now and then for a handful of friends was about it. But Sally had made him promise to continue the February event, even though it would be overshadowed by his recent sorrow. To Sally's way of thinking, Garrett needed to keep busy. And she was afraid if he dropped his old habits, he'd never pick them up again.

Now though, the party was only three weeks away, give or take a day or two. Would Clark still be around then? Despite Sally's prodding, the hot-tempered Garrett might cancel just to prevent Clark from attending. It would be a shame if an outsider ruined it for everyone else.

But you're also an outsider, an inner voice reminded. Jan quickly brushed the thought aside. Like Clark, she was a recent arrival, but—unlike him—she hadn't come trying to make people unhappy, trying to change lives. There was a big difference between her and Clark Brennan.

Speak of the devil, Jan passed Clark as she walked back to the ranch house. He looked solemn, confirming that either he was irritated with her or that he and Garrett did have words over the proposed outing—or both. Clark merely nodded as they passed, his dour expression causing Jan to worry more about B.J.

Garrett was sequestered in his study when Jan passed the room. The door was slightly ajar and through the opening she could see him gazing out the window, watching his grandson and the man who'd thoughtlessly intruded in the midst of their grief. The slump of Garrett's shoulders as the two nudged their horses toward the pasture, the sadness on his face, made Jan want to cry, and she resented Clark all the more.

CHAPTER FOUR

JAN went home, did a load of laundry and was preparing a crust for apple cobbler when she remembered they were out of sugar. Another trip to the grocery was needed.

Even though Sally kept insisting she was fully recovered, Jan stopped by the post office to check on her. She didn't want her aunt overdoing it and suffering a relapse. It turned out to be a bad decision.

Clark was there, sitting on one of the metal stools, talking with Sally as friendly as you please. Obviously the Brennan charm was not a total myth, because her aunt was giving him her undivided attention. Jan wanted to backtrack right out the door but there was no chance of that. Sally had already spied her.

"Hi, hon. Look who's here. Clark came in to mail a letter and I convinced him to stay for a cup of coffee while I take a quick break."

He raised his cup to Jan.

"Short ride," Jan chided, casting a disapproving glance at Clark. Obviously he'd soon tired of his son's company. They couldn't have been out more than an hour.

Clark tapped his watch. "On his grandfather's instructions—seems B.J. had a dental appointment. Is that a satisfactory excuse or do you want to give me another tongue-lashing?"

"Jan," Sally interrupted, before her niece could snipe back, "take off your coat and sit down. Let me get you a cup, too."

"Don't bother with the coffee. I know you don't have much time to spare." Jan sent another meaningful glance in Clark's direction. "I only wanted to say hello. I need to pick up some sugar and get back to the cobbler I'm making."

"Jan's a wonderful cook," Sally said to Clark, then turned back to her niece. "But I'll have to eat cobbler tomorrow. Remember, I've got that quilting party at Evelyn's tonight and she's serving dinner."

"No problem," Jan said. "Enjoy yourself and don't rush home on my account. See you later. Goodbye, Mr. Brennan."

"Oh, surely not goodbye." He slid off the stool. "I'll come with you. Carry the sugar." He followed her out of the post office and draped an arm across her shoulder as they crossed the street.

Jan shrugged his arm away. "What are you up to now? I'll not have you toying with Aunt Sally."

Clark chuckled. "I thought I was toying with you." The arm came back around her shoulder.

Jan stopped abruptly and backed away from his proprietary grip. "Cut that out. I don't want to be the object of gossip or conjecture. And that's precisely what will happen if you keep on this way. Surely you have something to do besides bothering me."

"Am I bothering you?"

"You know darn well—" She caught herself. "I'm not one of your groupies and I don't appreciate all this...this..."

"Male interest? I can't believe the local hot shots haven't shown you plenty of interest. Does it always make you this uncomfortable?"

"I'm not uncomfortable, I'm aggravated. Why don't you just leave me alone and concentrate on your son?"

"He's with his grandfather. I believe they said something about hamburgers for supper. So since Sally Mac has plans for this evening, too, why don't you have dinner with me? We can drive into Temple if you like."

"I don't like. As I said earlier, *goodbye*, Mr. Brennan."

Jan expected more argument, but he just grinned and headed back into the post office. She picked up the sugar and drove on home, all the while nervously contemplating Clark charming her aunt further and Sally Mac's imagination running rampant.

Clark's behavior didn't make sense after the virulence between them earlier in the day. What did he hope to gain by all this unwelcome attention? And why was she letting him get under her skin? She hated to admit that there was something about Clark that made her feel more alive, more vital. *Sex appeal. Plain old sex appeal. He has it in spades and any woman would be affected*. It was only natural. But if Clark thought he could use that appeal to make her compromise her principles, then he was sadly mistaken.

The bubbling dessert was cooling on the kitchen table and Jan had pulled out the ingredients for tuna salad sandwiches when a knock at the door startled her. She wasn't expecting anyone. And even though Valentine folks felt free to drop in unannounced, she knew that most of Sally's friends would be at the quilting party.

She was dismayed to discover Clark standing at the door. He was clutching a bottle of wine, which he handed to her as he brazenly strolled inside, uninvited. "Come in and make yourself comfortable," she said, her tone expressing a total lack of welcome.

"I won't stay long," he answered, nonchalantly shrugging out of his bomber jacket and pitching it across the back of the sofa. He was wearing crisp jeans and a long-sleeved black shirt buttoned at the neck. Apparently he had showered and shaved before coming over, because his hair was neatly combed and Jan detected a faint smell of cologne. She had to concede that he looked gorgeous.

And his appraisal of her also indicated approval. For an instant, she was happy that she'd dressed as she had, in mauve silk lounging pajamas. Then she remembered this man was her nemesis—not someone she wanted to impress. *He could have seen me at my worst. Who would care*? Still, she couldn't stop herself from running a hand across her hair as she closed the front door.

She hoped he wouldn't jump to the wrong conclusions. These pajamas had been donned not for glamour, but for comfort and only because all her sweats were in the laundry. Silk lounging pajamas were a part of her past, misfits in her life in Valentine.

Yet it had been impossible to wear them without also brushing her hair to a glossy sheen and touching up her makeup. Jan refused to validate the imp in her head that said she'd dressed this way in the hope of seeing Clark. Such a thought was intolerable.

"We'll need a couple of glasses," he said. "I thought a toast was in order—and a thank-you."

"I'm afraid I don't understand."

"B.J. said you suggested we talk. While we were riding and more so later, we did just that. I think it's helped us both and I wanted to show you that I'm grateful for the assistance."

"If you're so grateful, why didn't you mention it this afternoon?"

"I didn't know then that you were the one responsible for his opening up. Like I said, thank you."

"You're welcome," she answered grudgingly. "Although there was no need to return all the way into town to tell me." She handed the wine bottle back to him. "And this really isn't necessary, either. What I did was for B.J.'s benefit, not yours."

He laughed. "Still the prickly pear, aren't we? Surely we can share a toast. Maybe you'll even make a sandwich for me."

"I most certainly will not. We're not eating together and we're not sharing a drink." Jan knew she was behaving badly, but she couldn't stop herself. His mere presence sent her into a frenzy.

"Why do I irritate you so?" he asked insightfully. "Do you hate my after-shave? Am I using the wrong deodorant? Well, no matter. We need to talk, too, and I'm determined that's exactly what we're going to do." He walked past her, heading toward the kitchen. "I'll just find the glasses myself."

Jan stood there nonplussed as Clark wandered off into the kitchen, quickly returning with two juice glasses. "By the way, your aunt and I had a nice chat this afternoon. She's the most reasonable person I've met in town so far."

"I'm sure your approval will mean a lot to her," Jan said waspishly.

"I'm sure," he agreed with equal sarcasm. "My only complaint about her is that she doesn't have wine goblets. Or a corkscrew." He sat on the couch and took a Swiss Army Knife from his pocket. Managing to extract the cork from the bottle, he poured the wine, and handed a glass to Jan.

Resignedly, she sat down in a lounge chair. "So what was it you wanted to discuss?"

Clark gave her a studied gaze. "I was optimistic after our talks that I'd made some inroads with my son. I hoped to do the same with you. You're a puzzle to me." He took a sip of wine, his eyes peering over the rim of the glass to meet hers. "At first, I blamed your attitude toward me on Garrett. Now I'm not so sure it's all his doing. There's another agenda at work here. Either you come clean or I may resort to using my contacts for a bit of research on you."

"What...what do you mean?" A chill ran down Jan's spine. What exactly did he plan on researching? Had something come up about Glen?

"I mean I'm curious. The people here know everything about everyone. Yet other than your being Sally Mac's recently divorced niece, you're almost a lady of mystery. That piques my interest all the more—even though a woman like you is just naturally interesting. But that chip you're carrying around—wow. I want to find out why you're so down on me. Especially since you don't even know me."

"I care about B.J., that's all. But if it'll appease you, I'll try to be more accepting."

"Accepting doesn't seem to be part of your makeup from what I've seen to date."

"Have it your way," she snapped, then set her glass on the table and rose. "Excuse my bluntness and my lack of hospitality, but I've had enough of you for a while. You've been rude and objectionable from the first day we met."

He appeared intrigued by her outburst. "Interesting criticism. You could be describing yourself. Now that we've discovered we have something in common, you might as well sit back down while I finish my wine." He took another swallow. "And while we're sitting, maybe we can discover what other traits we share."

Silently she took her seat. The smirk on his face was infuriating, but she knew she might as well let him go at his own pace if she was ever to get rid of him.

He eyed her and something in his gaze indicated he was amused. "Let's start with Saturday," he said. "I don't know why you're so put out about it. All I did was flirt a little with a pretty woman." His stare changed into a questioning one. "Since when is that a sin?"

"It—ah—" Jan couldn't get out a reply. She was feeling inwardly pleased that he'd called her pretty, yet was berating herself for being such a wimp, having such a girlish reaction to the compliment. "Like I said..." She paused a moment to recover her composure. "I care about B.J. You hadn't seen him in over a year, but instead of spending time with him Saturday morning you were in town making moves on the first woman you saw."

"Definitely not the *first* one. There was Annette at the diner, a couple of her waitresses, those elderly twins that live in the apartment over Neumann's Grocery, and Mrs. Neumann herself. You were at least the seventh woman I saw that morning."

"For all I know you were cozying up to all of them, too."

"Are you jealous?"

"Don't be ridiculous, and quit changing the subject. We were talking about B.J."

"I believe there's a lot more to your attitude than B.J. You care about him all right. But now that I've thought about it, you've been adamant that you didn't know I was his father when we first met. Yet, your animosity was evident even then. No, there's more to this than just my son." He took a final sip of wine and leaned forward, resting his elbows on his knees. "Maybe the question I should be asking is whether you hate all men as much as you hate me? Has one bad experience soured you on the entire sex?"

Jan nervously twisted her glass between her hands, wondering how she'd managed to be so transparent. Except for Garrett and Sally, no one in Valentine knew much about her problems in Los Angeles, nor had any details about the sad end to her marriage. But, like he'd said, Clark had contacts. He might have already come upon something. Or was he merely fishing for information? "No comment," she said.

"Your aunt told me you've only lived here a few months. And you don't talk like a native. There's none of that Texas twang. In fact, your voice sounds professionally trained—almost like a performer's. Are you famous, a big star who's afraid of being unmasked—and, if so, what are you doing playing schoolteacher in Valentine?"

"I assure you I'm not famous." *At least not the kind of fame you're talking about.*

"Then where did you come from and how come the locals know so little about you? I haven't probed, but it seems they don't share much about Jan Armstrong. Is it your *real* name, or an alias? Could you be in a witness protection program?"

"Quit being fanciful. I'm from the West Coast, L.A., if you must know. I did a show there for preschoolers on public television." She might as well tell him. Thanks to a proud aunt, that was no secret in town. People must have assumed Clark already knew.

"To make a long story short, I lost my job and came to Valentine to lick my wounds while I decided what to do next. My father and aunt grew up here, so this seemed as good a place as any."

"You lost your job? Was it because of a man?"

She was surprised at the question. "Well, yes, you might say that."

"Ah, and that's what has made you so contemptuous of all males between twenty and sixty."

Jan could have kicked him—and herself, too. Why did she have to go and volunteer anything? Clark had cleverly thrown out some bait and she'd snapped it right up. Now she had to undo the damage she'd created or else he might make good on his threat to investigate her and learn even more than the bits and pieces he had.

Jan took a deep breath, trying to regain the upper hand. "Quit trying to analyze me like some amateur psychologist. The story's simple and pretty dull," she fibbed. "I lost a teaching position that I really loved, but not to a male. The end. And I'd prefer not to get into it anymore, if you don't mind."

"But I do mind. You're not talking to an amateur psychologist but to an old news hound, which means I'm naturally inquisitive...I want to hear the whole story with every comma intact. Despite what you say about dull, I know an overabridged version of a tale when I hear one. There's a lot of good stuff that you left out."

"Maybe, or maybe not," she said, forgetting her goal of appeasement. "Whichever, it's none of your business. I'm not a subject and you're not on assignment, so I suggest you focus on your son instead of me. Don't you have enough problems without trying to take on more?"

He placed his tumbler on a handy table, then got up, coming over to rest his hands on the arms of the chair, trapping her. "But you're such a *fetching* problem." He trailed a finger down her cheek and Jan slapped it away.

Clark studied her for a moment. "I'm not used to women bristling like a hedgehog when I come near them, so I can't help wondering why you react like you do. Believe it or not, most women seem to enjoy my attention."

"That's their problem. And I'm not most women." She pushed Clark away from her and stood up, carefully managing limited bodily contact with him. She pulled herself as tall as she could considering her lack of height and crossed her arms defensively.

"There's that schoolmarm pose, again, although that outfit isn't a bit schoolmarmish. You look like you're ready to give me another lecture."

"It appears you *need* a few lectures," she shot back, now wishing she did have on her sweats. "What's with you, anyway? Either you're dallying with me or trying to manipulate me. Is all this attention because of my position as B.J.'s teacher? Are you trying to gain my support against Garrett?"

"Is there any possibility I *could* gain your support?" His look was skeptical.

"Not really," she admitted. "So why don't you quit trying."

"For the record, I wasn't trying to sway your allegiance. I merely thought that perhaps I should give you some of the background, that maybe then you'd understand."

"I already know all that's necessary." Some part of Jan warned her she was being unfair again, but she couldn't bear to listen to Clark anymore. It was almost a matter of self-preservation. She felt much safer keeping him at arm's length. "Why don't you admit that you wouldn't allow fatherhood to interfere with your career and jet-set life-style?"

"So you have it all sorted out? I should have known I'd get nowhere with you. You're operating from Garrett's script. Are you also filling the role of surrogate daughter now that Toni's gone? Or is the relationship between you and Garrett closer...more intimate than that? Since you're B.J.'s teacher—for now, anyway—I feel I have the right to know."

"Why you insulting, low-minded idiot! Will you grab on to any insane notion? How could you possibly think there's anything...anything improper...between Garrett and me?"

"There has to be *some* rationale for your unquestioning loyalty."

"Well, you're grasping at straws. There's not a shred of evidence for such an accusation."

"Are you sure? According to the ranch hands, you've spent more than one night at the Lazy M."

"And you've decided it's something sexual?"

"It could be. Who are you dressed up for tonight, anyway?" His eyes gave another assessment of her lounging outfit.

"I don't owe you any explanations. You have a dirty mind, Mr. Brennan, and it's definitely time for you to go, before I...I..." She grabbed for the phone and waved it toward him. "Do I have to call the Lazy M and get a rescue squad over here?"

Clark raised a hand in a gesture of giving in. "Calm down. You don't have to tell me again. I'm out of here. Maybe I was wrong about you and Garrett. But I plan to find out why you treat me like I'm carrying some new form of plague. And that's not a threat—it's a promise." With his jacket slung over his shoulder, he strode out.

Jan leaned back against the door listening while the car motor started and Clark pulled out of the driveway. Her pulse was beating rapidly. She felt like a small, threatened animal—a hedgehog, perhaps, as Clark had suggested, and she tried to calm herself. It wouldn't take long for Clark to learn all about the mess with Glen. Not from anyone here—since only Sally and Garrett knew—but Clark-the-reporter with his access to newspaper and network staffers, could get information quite handily. If he really wanted to find out about Jan Armstrong, he would.

She sighed in frustration. Maybe she should have tried to diffuse his interest by candidly telling him everything in the first place—hoping he would leave her alone. But she couldn't do it—even the thought of rehashing the past made her tired. She had come to Valentine to put everything behind her and was finally beginning to get over the heartache; now Clark was stirring it up all over again. B.J. probably felt the same way.

B.J. Suddenly Jan recalled Clark's words. "You're B.J.'s teacher *for now anyway*." Would Clark actually remove B.J. from her tutoring? Jan wanted to believe there was no possibility of that, yet she knew she could be deluding herself. *Trust Garrett to take care of it*, she tried to convince herself, but she didn't feel reassured. Clark was apparently prepared to pull out all the stops—even to the point of linking her and Garrett romantically. It was ludicrous, of course, but Jan had been through too many emotional mine fields to gain any comfort from that. The only thing that would lift her spirits was to see the rear bumper of Clark's car on its way out of town.

CHAPTER FIVE

MUCH to Jan's disappointment, she awoke to a spectacular sunrise and the promise of a clear, beautiful day. She'd been praying for a record-setting blizzard, or at the very least, enough of the white stuff to make the roads impassable. That was to be her justification for not going out to the ranch, but evidently she couldn't depend on the weather as a protective buffer against Clark. Although snow was falling in the Texas Panhandle, the winter storm had stalled north of Wichita Falls, so the predicted flurries hadn't materialized. *Rats*!

Normally Jan loved her tutoring job. Usually she was anxious to get to the ranch. The thought of having to deal with Clark had changed all that. She dreaded another encounter, and for a variety of reasons. For starters, her awareness of Clark as a man—an attractive, desirable man—confounded and disturbed her. Secondly, his curiosity about her past threatened her current existence.

But it was those impertinent remarks concerning her relationship with Garrett she found most troubling at the moment. Merely remembering them caused her blood pressure to rise. *How dare Clark accuse her of something so asinine*!

She'd considered informing Garrett of Clark's insinuations, then discarded the notion after she thought it through. Garrett's knowing wouldn't accomplish much except to make him even angrier with Clark.

There was no point in turning up the heat on an already-boiling pot.

Talking to Sally wasn't an alternative, either. Unless Jan swore her to secrecy, her aunt would probably feel an obligation to tell Garrett herself. Either way it would put Sally in an untenable situation and she'd be where Jan was now—caught in the middle of someone else's war.

It was best for both women to stay out of Garrett's and Clark's problems—*if* they could. Remaining neutral was becoming more difficult for Jan. One more disparaging remark from Clark and she'd have to do something. She'd vowed upon leaving Los Angeles never to be walked on again. She'd call his hand even if it did result in more tension between him and Garrett.

"He's probably been up all night trying to dig up as much dirt on me as he can," she muttered to herself on the drive toward the Montgomery ranch. "So what?" she continued, answering herself. "There's nothing he can unearth that could hurt me now. My past may be a big secret in Valentine, but the people here probably wouldn't hold it against me if they found out. So let him dig. I'm not going to worry about it another minute." The words were mere bluster, though, and Jan couldn't get her thoughts off the challenge from Clark the evening before.

Much to Jan's dismay, Garrett's Ford pickup was gone when she pulled up in front of the ranch house. Even though she'd decided not to tell him about the confrontation with Clark, she still wished for the security of his presence. Especially since the rental car, a black Pontiac Jan now recognized as belonging to Clark, was parked there. Oh, well, she'd just make a beeline for the classroom and get ready for today's lessons. Maybe that way, she could avoid Clark.

No such luck. She was erasing an arithmetic problem left over from yesterday's aborted lesson when Clark stuck his head in. "B.J.'s finishing breakfast," he announced from the door of the room. "He'll be along in a minute."

Jan nodded and turned back to the chalkboard easel.

"And in case you're wondering, Garrett isn't here."

She nodded again, not turning around.

"So there's no one for you to tattle to."

She waited a moment, then nodded a third time. Intuition told her that her lack of communication was annoying Clark. She could only hope so anyway.

He walked over and inserted his face between Jan and the chalkboard. "Now, *Ms. Armstrong*, as cool as you're trying to be, I know you can't wait to blab to Garrett about last night."

Jan backed away. "What makes you think that?"

"I just figured it'd be one more entry for his list of grievances against me, a list I'm sure you concur with totally."

"Are you about to make a point here? If you're trying to get me not to talk to him, I promise you this isn't the way to go about it."

"Is there a way?"

"I'm not sure," she said, flipping a piece of chalk from one hand to the other.

"Okay," he replied. "I concede that I was out of line. My purpose in stopping by last night was to thank you—not insult you."

"If so, you missed the mark."

"I know and I regret it."

"Can I view this as an apology?"

He paused before answering. "One's apparently warranted. Also, I need to ask a favor." He shrugged his shoulders and grinned sheepishly. The kind of grin that almost made Jan agree to any request before he voiced it.

"While I'm admitting to being out of line, I would appreciate your not sharing my foolishness with B.J.'s grandfather. Believe it or not, I want to get along with him. And I'd like to get along with you, too."

When pigs fly, Jan nearly replied, but instead managed to answer, "We'll see." Clearly Clark had spent some time evaluating his rash comments and had decided it was worth an apology to keep from provoking Garrett further.

"By the way," he said, "I've learned a few interesting things about you from some of my sources."

Jan's hackles began to rise. So much for his trying to make amends. What did he think he could do—blackmail her into cooperating? If so, he was in for a big disappointment. If incited, she might just talk to Garrett after all. And once she started, she'd say plenty, giving her opinion loud and clear. She'd tell all the world that not only was Clark Brennan a lousy father, but also an extortion-loving bully with a mind in the gutter. That's what she'd say—if it became necessary, that is.

"Aren't you interested in what I heard?"

"Not really. I knew it was just a matter of time anyway. People in the information business love to disclose anything that falls under the heading of gossip. So you found out about my ex-husband's legal problems, about the trial...it's all public information—so what?"

Clark shook his head. "Actually my sources were the ranch hands and what I found out is that you are a great cook, just like Sally Mac said. They tell me your fudge is the best in town. But I appreciate your divulging those other tidbits to me."

Jan could have run into the nearest wall head-first. Here she was worrying about him finding out all about her and she'd saved him the trouble by popping off and volunteering the information herself. *Was there no way she could control her own big mouth*?

"What happened with your ex-husband, Jan? With your marriage?"

"None of your business."

"Is he the reason you freeze up whenever I come near?"

"I don't freeze up."

"Yes, you do." His blue eyes held her captive. "But we won't talk about that now. I'm sorry you were hurt."

She shrugged.

"Divorce is rotten. But it's even worse when children are involved. Like B.J."

"Are you trying to tell me how fortunate it was I didn't have children? Because if you are, I don't agree with you. I came away from my marriage empty-handed when I would have adored having a son or daughter to love."

"I came away empty-handed, too. I had a double loss."

"Partly by choice."

Clark ignored the gibe. "Like I said, I'm sorry you suffered a broken heart."

"Heart's mend, so I'm told," she said dismissively. She didn't want Clark's compassion, or his pity.

"But yours hasn't?"

"I really don't want to talk about this." When was Clark going to get that through his thick head?

"Okay. For now, anyway. I'm heading into town. I'll send B.J. to you on my way out."

When teacher and pupil took a midmorning break to check on the animals, Clark was long gone. They played with the kittens, petted Speckles, then Jan sat on the step and watched B.J. as he repeatedly raced between the house and the corral to release some little boy energy.

Afterward they returned to schoolwork. During the half hour set aside for art, they made a valentine list and sketched numerous designs. Tomorrow they'd write some verses, and the day after it'd be time to cut out red and pink construction paper hearts and add lacy doilies and fancy ribbons.

B.J. seemed calmer today, as though expressing his feelings to Clark had purged some of his pent-up resentment. The improved attitude couldn't simply be attributed to the fact that his father was away for the present. B.J. hadn't been distraught earlier or seemed to mind that it was Clark who sent him to the classroom.

On the way home, Jan ducked into the post office. "How's it going?"

Sally rolled her eyes to the ceiling. "Too hectic for words. The mail load today was especially heavy and everyone is having to work late."

"Can I help?"

"Would you mind picking up supper for the crew—sandwiches or hamburgers?"

"I'll do better than that," Jan said. "I'll fix a meal myself and then come back to give another pair of hands."

Sally gave a grateful sigh. It was an offer she couldn't refuse.

"What to cook?" Jan mumbled to herself as she crossed the street to the grocery. A glance at the black rental car parked in front almost caused her to change her mind and forget shopping. Surely there was food to select from at home. Or she could buy the hamburgers after all.

Then she chided herself for being ridiculous. In a town this small you ran into friends and family and even enemies wherever you went. There was no way she could successfully dodge Clark and she might as well stop trying.

Along with several other patrons, Clark waved to her as she entered, his attention then returning to the domino game he'd joined at a corner table. As she picked up the items for an enchilada casserole, Jan couldn't help but overhear the conversation between the players and their observers. Clark was a television star and the locals were plainly enjoying having someone of his stature in town. Good heavens, thought Jan, they're acting like Frank Sinatra—or better yet, considering this was Valentine, country legend Willie Nelson—had sat down to play with them.

"Then the artillery began shelling the hotel," Clark said. "Glass breaking, giant holes appearing in the walls, sirens screaming . . ." He looked up to see her listening in. "Want to join us?"

Before she could answer, one of the men prompted Clark, "And what happened then?"

"Well, about that time I got hit in the arm." He rolled up his sleeve and showed them a scar.

"Give me a break," Jan mumbled to herself as she walked away to begin her shopping. *You'd think the man would affect a little modesty. I'm surprised he's not peddling autographed pictures*. But at least he hadn't hounded her like that last time she'd been in the store. Now that she thought about it, this was the first instance since they'd met that he'd treated her just like anyone else. For that she was grateful. Or so she told herself. But somewhere in the back of her mind, she perversely felt ignored.

Jan couldn't dispel the disgruntled feeling even after she'd arrived home. She tried to convince herself that this was a sign the relationship between her and Clark had improved—at least to the point they could be civil to one another. But it was likely a temporary phenomenon. Since it usually took less than three minutes for them to start quarreling, she'd be overly optimistic to expect anything more.

Fortunately, she had plenty besides Clark to occupy her mind this afternoon. She'd toss a salad, bake the casserole and a lemon pie for dessert—then in the evening, she'd postmark cards for Sally. It'd be to her advantage to stay out of the house. Insurance against any more nocturnal visits from a certain nosy reporter.

Garrett's truck was in evidence when she arrived at the ranch the next day, but this time his Chrysler was gone. Thankfully, Clark's vehicle was also absent. Jan said hello to Rue Nell in the kitchen, then went straight to the classroom.

The morning passed quickly and Jan was standing by her desk, preparing to leave, when Clark reappeared. He jiggled his car keys in his pocket. "Garrett's not back yet?"

"No."

"I understand he went to Temple. Do you know why?"

Jan hadn't realized the rancher was on the road. B.J. hadn't said anything. Sally and Rue Nell hadn't mentioned it, either. But even if she was aware of his whereabouts, no explanation was owed to Clark. "You should ask him yourself when he gets back," she said, dodging a direct answer.

"I believe that you know exactly what he's up to. You're just not telling me."

"I might have an idea," Jan answered, remembering Garrett's resolve to talk to a lawyer. "Then again, I'm not sure." She stuffed a sheaf of lesson plans into her briefcase. "You'll still have to find out from him."

"That confirms it," he said.

"Confirms what?"

"That what I heard this morning at Neumann's is true. Garrett's up to something. And I suspect you're a party to it." The car keys jiggled faster.

Although they shouldn't have, his accusations surprised Jan. It was just as she'd thought. The cease-fire was temporary. After yesterday's momentary truce, the hostilities between them were reopened.

"Whatever are you talking about?"

"Don't bother playing dumb. Garrett's activities didn't appear to be much of a secret in town—a couple of people acted surprised I was 'still round'—the implication being that he would have gotten rid of me by now. The grocer seemed to think Garrett had gone to Temple about a legal matter. From the way everybody talked, *I'm* the legal matter."

"Neumann's Grocery is a gossip mill," Jan said.

"Yes, and a pretty good one. Thanks to all those chatty citizens, I have a good idea what Garrett's up to."

Jan didn't answer.

"He's getting advice on how to separate me from my son—permanently."

Again Jan made no response.

"If I thought I was going to ease my way into Garrett's good graces, I appear to be sadly mistaken."

Jan knew she should go home right then. Continuing this conversation would just pull her deeper into a problem all common sense told her to stay out of. There was no way she could mediate Clark's and Garrett's differences, however much she wanted to help B.J. But despite her resolve to remain on the sidelines, she impulsively asked, "So what do you plan to do?"

"I've a few things in mind. I've already done one of them."

"And what's that?" She wasn't sure she wanted to know.

"Employed a bit of chess strategy. Checkmate."

"I don't understand." She sat down in the swivel chair and Clark perched on the corner of the desk, looking down at her.

"I'm never going to stay away from B.J. again. In case Garrett has other ideas, I decided to make it more difficult for him."

"How?"

"By becoming his next-door neighbor. I've finished negotiations to buy the adjoining ranch—we signed the papers this morning."

"The Phillips' place? You talked Zeke Phillips into selling?"

"Well, I guess the real estate agent talked him into it. I merely put out the word that I wanted to buy a spread. Phillips contacted me."

Jan put her hand to her face. "I don't believe my ears."

"What's the problem? I figured you'd be pleased by the purchase, that you'd think it would be good for B.J. After all, you're the one who accused me of not spending enough time with my son." He casually swung a Levi's-clad leg. "Who knows? With me on the scene, Garrett may even come around eventually."

"Don't bet on it. If you've been hoping that time will mend your fences with Garrett Montgomery, I suspect you've done something now to guarantee it never happens."

"What do you mean?"

"According to Aunt Sally, Garrett has coveted that property for thirty years—maybe longer. He's done everything short of get down on his hands and knees and beg Zeke Phillips to sell. But Zeke and Garrett had this grudge match going over Elaine, Garrett's wife. Apparently Zeke was in love with Elaine and thought Garrett stole her away from him. Garrett thought Zeke was trying to undermine his marriage. The two of them went from being friends to bitter rivals.

"And the dispute didn't end with Elaine's death. In fact, it got worse. That was when Zeke fenced off Garrett's access to the river. The Lazy M has water tanks and wells, so it wasn't a real problem. 'Just the principle of the thing,' Garrett says. Zeke Phillips would have gone broke before he'd let Garrett buy his land. Apparently he heard about you and Garrett and decided to exact a measure of revenge by letting you have it." She shook her head. "Looks like you've stepped into a rattlesnake nest. Garrett's going to be furious when he finds out you own it."

Clark's face darkened. "Well, that's tough! I've done everything I can to try and appease the man. Surely he'll be rational long enough to realize the property's all in the family now, so to speak. I assume the Montgomery place will come to B.J. someday, just like my land will. That means Garrett has nothing to lose."

"Maybe so, but I doubt he'll see it that way. He'll most likely decide that you're in league with Zeke, your only motive being to spite him."

"But why would he think such a thing? What could I possibly gain by aggravating him more than he already is?" Clark looked genuinely perplexed.

"I don't know," Jan answered wearily and glanced at her watch. "But I need to leave. I've got errands to run."

Clark might not be finished with their discussion, but without complaint he picked up her briefcase, walked her to the front door, then on to her car. He was apparently on his way out anyway—instead of returning to the house, he got in his car and followed her down the ranch drive, then they turned in opposite directions onto the farm road.

By Thursday, the town was buzzing with speculation about Clark's real estate acquisition. Jan was expecting him when Clark showed up on her doorstep that night. He hadn't been at the ranch during B.J.'s lessons so she guessed he'd be seeking her out sooner or later.

She'd almost decided her intuition had failed her by the time he arrived. It was late—almost ten—and Sally had gone to bed. Jan met him at the side door, by the carport. "What are you doing here *this* time?" she said, feigning a slight annoyance. Inwardly, she found herself suppressing a smile and wondered why. Surely she couldn't be glad to see him.

"Looking for a little privacy. I'd forgotten about small towns, how uncomfortable it can be as the center of attention."

"Considering your career choice, you ought to be used to attention." He hadn't minded yesterday, Jan thought, when he was playing to the audience at Neumann's Grocery. But that had been adoration, she remembered. Today was different. Apparently the town had gotten itself embroiled in the controversy between Clark and Garrett—and there was no question where the loyalty of most of the citizens lay. Still, she didn't accept privacy as the reason why Clark had sought her out, why he was now sitting across the table from her in Sally's kitchen. "Isn't the Lazy M private enough?" She got up from the table and picked up the coffeepot, gesturing to Clark with it. He nodded.

"The ranch may be the least private place in town. The way he was hollering, every hand in the bunk house could hear Garrett's reaction when I told him about buying the Phillips property. I still don't know why it's such a big deal. If he wants the damn ranch,

I'll sell it to him. I found this one and I can find another."

Jan might not have grown up around Valentine, but she'd quickly grasped the psyches of men like Garrett Montgomery. He didn't want the land anymore—he just wanted to keep his grandson and expunge Clark from their lives.

"Well, aren't you going to enlighten me on what to do next?"

"I didn't realize I'd become such a valued advisor." She scooped coffee into a paper filter and poured water into the coffee maker.

Clark held up his hands. "Pax. Help me, Jan. I really do want to understand the old man."

"I doubt that I can help. For one thing, I'm puzzled by what you've done. You could have achieved your purpose of staying close to B.J. by getting a house in town. You didn't have to buy a ranch. Do you even know the first thing about running one?"

"Not as much as I'd like, nor as much as I plan to know. But I'm not some dumb greenhorn, either. I *am* from Texas in case you didn't know. I grew up in San Angelo, right in the heart of ranching country. I can ride and rope and I've even tamed a wild horse or two. Not that I'd want to do it again."

She did know he was from Texas. A time or two, she could hear traces of what must have been his former accent. But the ranching background—that was news to her.

"The fact that you've some experience is all well and good, but as far as appeasing Garrett, your buying that property is like putting out a fire with gasoline. All you've done is make the conflict bigger and hotter."

"I hope not."

Jan poured them cups of coffee. "I hope not, too," she said, sitting back down.

Clark reached across the table and took her hand. She resisted the inclination to yank it away, even though the gesture made her uneasy. The two sat silently, drinking the coffee, Clark not saying anything else or doing anything but continuing to hold her hand. When his cup was empty, he released his grip and stood. "Thanks for listening. I'd better say good-night now."

Jan saw him out, watching through the screen door as he climbed into his car. As she dressed for bed, her thoughts were fixated on Clark's visit. Was he seeking her out only because of her connection to B.J.? Or was it possible that he, too, sensed some unspoken tie between them, a tie that Jan was trying so hard to discount?

Had Garrett been successful in his trip to Temple? He was gone a long time—usually his excursions were limited to a few short hours. Maybe he'd been delayed because he heard something that would cause him to be more yielding as far as Clark was concerned. But Jan doubted it.

Most likely he'd already started whatever legal proceedings he had planned and if she were guessing, she'd say that Garrett was going to be more determined than ever to get rid of Clark Brennan after this latest news. Why, suddenly, did the idea not seem as palatable as before?

CHAPTER SIX

AS SOON as the alarm rang the next morning, Jan was up. She listened to the news on the radio while sipping coffee and dressing. Once again she was disappointed there would be no bad weather. The storm front had moved eastward and the weekend forecast was for fair skies.

"Coward," she called herself, feeling tension in the pit of her stomach as she contemplated what she'd encounter today. Oh, well, she thought, might as well get out to the ranch and see what's happening.

The Lazy M had temporarily escaped meteorological problems, but another storm was raging when she pulled up in front of the house—not the expected fight between Clark and Garrett, but a Richter scale tantrum from B.J. Even before she rang the bell, she could hear him yelling.

"No! No! I don't want to wear that. I want my green shirt, the one with the dinosaurs!"

Jan peered through the glass panes. She could see the child sitting cross-legged on the floor, his eyes red-rimmed. Clark was standing over him. Apparently the tantrum had been going on for some time. She tried the knob. The door was unlocked so she quietly entered.

"You heard Rue Nell say it was in the laundry," Clark tried to reason. "You can wear it tomorrow. Or later on today after it's washed."

"I don't want it tomorrow." B.J. flung out a small booted foot and kicked his father's ankle. Jan saw Clark's neck redden in anger as he reached down and rubbed the spot. "Kicking is not allowed," he said sternly.

B.J.'s response was to kick out at Clark again, but his aim was off this time. He began crying loudly.

Clark looked around, suddenly aware of Jan watching them. "Any suggestions?" he asked under his breath. "This has lasted for half an hour. And before you say anything, I've already tried ignoring him."

"Has Garrett talked to him?" she whispered back.

"Oh, no. His only words were 'You're his daddy. Take care of it.' Then he stalked off to his study."

"Why don't I take care of it this time?" Jan suggested, easing out of her jacket. Clark raised his hands as though to say she was welcome to it, but he didn't leave.

"Go," Jan instructed, pointing toward the stairway, and even though Clark obviously wanted to see the scene through, he did as she said.

Jan knelt beside the boy. "Aren't you ashamed of yourself for acting this way?" He didn't answer, but his face did appear somewhat contrite. Jan put her arm around him.

"Are you unhappy because your father and grandfather argued yesterday?"

The child nodded.

"Let's go to the school room so you can tell me about it."

"But I don't have a shirt on."

"We'll worry about that later."

It took her almost an hour to calm the child. They read stories and listened to music. Not a productive use of time in terms of schoolwork, but obviously what was necessary. In no way would B.J. be able to concentrate on math or geography. Eventually he talked a bit about what he'd overheard. Between the Clark-Garrett warfare itself and the gossip of the ranch staff, the child was overwhelmed. Jan was furious at both men. Whatever their differences, the two needed to start focusing on how much their open conflict was distressing the boy.

Each professed to love him, to want him. Then why couldn't they understand that they weren't competing for some inanimate object? If they didn't stop fighting, they were going to destroy the object of their devotion.

The past few weeks she'd been optimistic that B.J. was making headway. Now she worried whether that progress had totally disappeared. He could stand just so much stress and he'd already suffered more lately than an adult should have to handle, much less a child. Before she left today, she intended to give both men a piece of her mind about their feuding. She ought to have done so days ago.

When lunchtime arrived, Jan took B.J. off to the kitchen. She had planned to search for Garrett, only to learn from Rue Nell that he'd gone into town. With that news, Jan began looking for Clark. She found him with the horses, pitching clean hay into their stalls. "Hello," she said.

He nodded, but continued working. Tension was evident in his movements as he finished with the hay, then picked up a currying comb. Jan watched as he vigorously groomed a black stallion. Good thing horses had tough hides, she thought, or he'd be rubbing the poor animal raw.

Clark was obviously working off days of frustration. Once or twice, he wiped his brow on the sleeve of his denim shirt, then he pulled out a handkerchief from the pocket of his Levi's and mopped his face. Eventually she cleared her throat, but he still didn't turn toward her or openly acknowledge her presence.

"Can we talk?" she said, trying to keep her thoughts together and her temper steady.

He turned, waving a hand in the air. "Do you mean talk... or am I supposed to listen to another dressing down? If that's it, I can tell you right now that I've had enough." He lay the currying comb on the ledge of the stall. "If it weren't for B.J., I'd be out of here by sundown."

"Was that the option Garrett offered?"

"In so many words. By the way, is he okay?"

Clark's glance toward the house confirmed that the "he" was B.J., not his grandfather.

"Better, I think. He can't go on like this, though. Surely you realize that."

"Do you think I like what's happening?"

"No, but you're not making it any better."

"Then you're saying the problems are all my fault."

"Not entirely, but—"

"Thank heaven for small favors. So they're just *mostly* my fault."

Jan resented his attitude. All she was trying to do was help. "Your fault or not, things were certainly simpler before you arrived."

"Well, too bad everybody's been inconvenienced. You'll just have to put up with me, though. And if I should leave—which I don't plan to—I wouldn't be going alone.'' The threat was implicit. Clark's legs were planted apart, a fist on each hip, his whole posture defiant, and Jan knew that nothing she said would make any difference at the moment. Besides, she was frightened. Scared that Clark, if pushed too far, would do something drastic, like steal away with B.J. And, if he did, what could anyone do about it? As Clark Brennan kept reminding everyone—he *was* B.J.'s father.

She might as well go on home. Maybe Sally would have some ideas. Maybe *she* could get through to these hardheaded men. *Somebody had to*. ''Believe what you will,'' she said to Clark, ''but I'm not trying to assess blame. Although you must admit there's plenty of it to go around. I'll see you next week.''

Pulling a meat loaf from the oven, Jan smiled at Sally who had just entered the kitchen. ''Rough day?'' she asked as Sally dropped into a chair and immediately took off her shoes.

''That's just the half of it. Been on my feet since seven. I feel like I've walked a thousand miles and handled a million pieces of mail. Would you believe there was even one card from Russia? I didn't realize they celebrated Valentine's Day there—do they?''

Jan smiled again. The whole town might be abuzz with the local Clark-Garrett gossip, but Sally was all wrapped up in her valentines. According to Jan's father, she'd been like that for years. ''I don't really know,'' she answered. ''Most of the countries where I lived as a child had some kind of observance.'' She moved from the store and pulled two plates from the cabinet.

"What do you think about the Phillips place?" Jan asked as she was setting the table. Between their work schedules and Sally's social outings with her friends, there hadn't been an opportunity for the two of them to talk in depth about Clark's buying the ranch.

"Everyone's surely twittering over it, especially about the friction between the two men. They expect Clark and Garrett to wage a high-noon showdown on Main Street. Garrett stopped by the post office earlier today. I was glad to see him—he hadn't visited since he got home from Temple. I was also glad everyone else had gone to lunch because he was howling like a wounded pup, so mad at Zeke—and Clark—that he couldn't see straight. What do you know about the situation?"

"Not much. According to Clark they had some pretty strong words."

"Did he tell you that this morning—or when he came by last night?"

Jan eyed Sally. She hadn't realized her aunt knew about Clark's visit. "Last night. As you might expect, B.J.'s pretty upset about it."

"Sounds like the grown-ups at the Montgomery ranch are the ones acting like kids. Well, Garrett always has had a temper. Speaks before he thinks sometimes."

Jan was surprised Sally wasn't defending her friend, but then she tended to be careful and objective, reluctant to take sides in other people's quarrels. When Sally saw wrong, however, she didn't hesitate to speak her piece. "I believe in calling a spade a spade," she often said.

"So what do you think?" Jan prompted, wanting more of her aunt's views, hoping she'd have an opening to suggest that Sally talk turkey to the men.

Sally slipped her feet back into her shoes. "I think I want to change into my bathrobe and slippers before we eat—if you don't mind. We can chat over supper."

As soon as they sat down for the meal, Jan posed the question again. "I, for one, am glad Clark's settling here," Sally told her. "It's best for everyone concerned."

"Are you serious?" Jan filled her plate with meat loaf, green beans, and a scoop of mashed potatoes.

"Dead serious. I figure Clark wouldn't have spent that kind of money buying Zeke's place unless he was fixing to stay a while. It relieves my mind that he's planning on taking over the care of B.J. I've been worried about Garrett. He's too old to be rearing a youngster." Sally gestured toward the meat loaf. "This is good, even better than usual."

"Did Garrett consult a lawyer?" Jan knew that Garrett's personal affairs were really none of her business and that too much knowledge would just keep her stewing, but she couldn't quell her curiosity. Especially after today.

"He sure did. He was riled up about that, too. In fact, it probably contributed to him throwing such a big fit over the land. The lawyer told him that, under the circumstances, his chances of getting custody of B.J. were slim."

"Then what is he going to do—give up?"

"My, no! When Garrett puts his mind to something, nothing gets in his way." Sally picked up a cornbread muffin and cut it in half. "He'll see another lawyer, and then another, until he finds one who tells him what he wants to hear. That Garrett Montgomery is one stubborn old goat."

Jan smiled inwardly. Sally's words were critical, but lovingly said, the affection obvious. That made Sally's position all the more curious. Knowing that her aunt cared deeply about B.J., too, Jan wondered how she could be so upbeat about the possibility of him ending up with Clark. She herself didn't feel the same generosity of spirit, or the confidence that the boy would be better off with his father.

The weekend was busy. Both Jan and Sally spent most of Saturday at the post office, then they devoted Sunday to church and visiting with Sally's friends. Conversations centered on two topics—Valentine's Day and the Montgomery-Brennan controversy.

Considering her previous contempt for the upcoming holiday, Jan amazed herself by the frequency with which she steered the talk in that direction. At least then the subject was nonthreatening. Whenever the patter was about Clark, Garrett or B.J., she couldn't prevent her stomach from knotting and her pulse rate from rising.

Early Monday morning, Garrett called to tell Jan that she didn't need to come out to the ranch that day. A horse sale was being held in Hillsboro and he wanted to take B.J. with him. *Likely, he just wants to get B.J. away from Clark*, she thought, but once again reminded herself that her opinions had best remain unspoken.

If she'd known earlier about the horse-buying excursion, she could have offered to help out at the post office, but Sally had already secured a full complement of workers, so now she wasn't needed.

She considered going back to bed, then changed her mind. Once more, snow was predicted, either by nightfall or certainly by Tuesday or Wednesday. The weatherman—not a bit embarrassed that he'd been so wrong before—had been adamant that the area wouldn't be bypassed during this go-round.

Finding herself the beneficiary of unexpected leisure, Jan decided to drive into Temple and run some errands before getting weatherbound. She hadn't been anywhere except in and around town and to the Montgomery ranch since she'd taken the tutoring job. And the last time she'd been to Temple was for Christmas shopping. She needed the break. It was possible that her fretting of late had been exacerbated by constant exposure to the problems around her.

Today she would visit the mall and pick up valentines to send to her parents, a family tradition which she felt obliged to uphold. No doubt her labors at the post office had caused her to put off the purchase, the idea of handling even more cards being particularly unappealing.

Yet now, unaccountably, she felt more enthusiastic. The likely reason was that she'd succumbed to the Valentine virus, become caught up in the observance, along with everyone else in town. Whatever.... She mentally made out a list for small gifts...one for Sally and B.J. Maybe something for Garrett and Sally's aides, too. Clark Brennan was a deliberate omission from her list.

The stores had just opened when Jan arrived at the mall. She took the opportunity to browse around. In the window of a store specializing in Western wear she spotted a dress. She hadn't planned to buy any clothes, but—what the heck? Except for a pair of jeans, she hadn't added to her wardrobe since she'd been in Valentine. Besides, this outfit was cherry red, with long sleeves and a prairie-styled skirt. It would be perfect for Garrett's Valentine's Day dance. On impulse, Jan went in and tried on the dress.

She hadn't thought about what to wear for the annual event. Actually she hadn't been sure she even wanted to go, so why did she feel so pleased about finding the dress? It wasn't the style she normally wore, nor something that would really be a useful addition to her wardrobe. And it was expensive, especially considering her dismal financial situation since the divorce. But she'd been saving her money since she'd arrived in Texas, and it was time she treated herself. The guilty feelings brushed aside, she headed toward the car to stash her purchase in the trunk.

Once outside the mall, she looked up to check the sky. It seemed as though the forecast might be accurate this time. Clouds were gathering, with only a few patches of blue visible.

Still, she wasn't too concerned just yet. There was plenty of time to make her card selections, look for presents, do more window-shopping and possibly eat a bite of lunch. As long as the storm held off, she had no reason to race back home.

The last person she expected to come upon in the toy store was Clark Brennan. She didn't recognize him at first glance, the man in the black Western hat and the sheepskin coat. He was standing in the electric train section holding up one miniature car after another. Then he turned his head.

Carrying the puzzles and books she'd picked out for B.J., she walked over his way. No point in acting like she hadn't seen him. She wouldn't be able to pass by him without being spotted anyway.

"Hi," she said.

"Well, hello."

"You've got new clothes." She gestured to the hat and coat.

"Do you approve?"

She nodded.

"Figured if I was going to be a Texas rancher, I might as well look the part. Just got them, in fact, tags are in my pocket. Now I'm trying to make some major decisions about cabooses. But what are you doing here?"

"Actually, shopping for your son," she answered. She showed her selections to him.

Clark studied the book. "Hmm...horses. Is this your choice or Garrett's?"

"Mine. B.J. *likes* horses. Is that all right with you?" Her voice had an edge.

"Of course. I shouldn't have implied anything. Blame it on a general bad mood."

"Garrett still giving you a rough time?"

Clark ran his fingers through his hair. "To put it mildly. Only his strong sense of Texas hospitality—or more likely, concern I'd take my son with me if I left—has kept him from kicking me out of the house. He's convinced I fast-talked Zeke Phillips into selling me the land to prevent him from getting it. To be honest, I thought you were exaggerating when you told me of Garrett's interest in the property and the bad blood between him and Zeke. I guess I owe you yet another apology."

Jan's suspicions were aroused. She couldn't help but be cautious whenever Clark became conciliatory.

But she didn't want to argue with him today. It had been too pleasant an outing to spoil with a disagreement. "I'm surprised you didn't hear about the feud before," she said. "It's certainly no secret around town—everyone knows. At the very least, I would have thought Toni had told you."

"You'd be amazed how rarely Toni and I talked about anything, especially her father, who was a sore subject in our marriage. He didn't exactly approve of me as husband material, even back then."

"Why not?" Jan pulled out her wallet and signaled to the salesclerk who was arranging a display of Barbie dolls.

"He thought I ought to get a *real* job. Television wasn't his idea of a stable profession. Odd coming from a man who got his start as a professional bull rider. But Garrett always thought my job was the root of our marriage problems."

Jan tended to think Garrett was right, but reminded herself that it would be best to steer the subject away from him. She was determined to let nothing ruin the day. "How did you get into television?"

"A degree in broadcast journalism from the University of Texas. Actually my TV career started in Dallas. That's where I met Toni. She was in town on a shopping spree at Neiman Marcus and a mutual friend introduced us. At first I thought it was just me her father didn't like, then later I wondered if anyone would have been good enough for his darling daughter."

The clerk came to ring up her purchase and Jan pulled out a couple of tens to pay. "So what are you going to do about the ranch?"

"Who knows? I tried the magnanimous route—and he brushed off my offer to sell him the property. I guess the land's tainted in his eyes. Or maybe he feels he'd be obligated to me."

Clark fiddled with a boxcar. The salesperson gift wrapped Jan's purchases, then turned to him. "Have you made up your mind, sir?"

"I need to think about it some." He turned to Jan. "How about lunch? You can help me decide what to buy while we eat."

A few days ago she would have turned him down without a pause, but today Clark seemed vulnerable, in need of company. The way he was agonizing over the train pieces somehow touched her. She hadn't the heart to turn him down. What harm would lunch do anyway? Apparently he was going to be around for a while and it would serve no purpose to perpetuate hostilities. Maybe by being less judgmental of his father, she could help B.J.

CHAPTER SEVEN

THEY went to Manuelitos, a Mexican restaurant located within the mall. Jan slid into one side of a shiny, red plastic booth and Clark sat across from her. "Iced tea?" he asked as the waitress approached.

"Fine," Jan agreed.

Clark held up two fingers and the waitress left to get their drinks. "I'd almost forgotten that Texans love their iced tea year round." He pushed a menu toward Jan.

She nodded in acknowledgment. "It could be twenty below zero," she said, "and people here would still demand it." She studied the menu. "Any recommendations?"

"No, I haven't been to this restaurant before. Pretty amazing considering how much I miss Tex-Mex food when I'm traveling." Clark opened his menu and started scanning the selections. "Thanks for joining me."

"Any time," she answered unconsciously.

"Any time?" His eyes twinkled.

"That's not exactly what I meant," Jan said, but for once, she didn't object to Clark's banter, nor his teasing smile, and she couldn't help but smile in return.

The waitress reappeared with their tea, a basket of tortilla chips and a bowl of picante sauce. Clark leaned toward Jan. "I'm going to hold you to it. Whenever

I have a Mexican-food attack, I'll expect you to come back here with me."

"Only if you pick up the check," she retorted, dunking a tortilla chip into the bowl of hot sauce. "If you're going to be so demanding, then you'll have to pay the price."

"You honestly believe I'd let a woman pay for her own dinner? Not in this part of the country, ma'am." He grinned again. "See how quickly I'm readjusting to the role of the macho Texas male."

"Oh, without a doubt, you've adjusted quite handily," Jan said, concentrating on how attractive he was today. His blue sports shirt emphasized his eyes, heightening their color to that of a clear summer sky. He needed a haircut, but the longer hair was rather nice, more wavy and even curling up a bit at the ends.

"So you think I'm macho?"

Jan's mind quickly returned to the subject at hand as she tabulated various meanings of the word—male, lusty, virile. "I hadn't given it much thought," she fibbed. "But the other women in the restaurant obviously think so." The hostess and waitress and a couple of the female diners had been openly admiring. Jan couldn't squelch a frisson of pleasure that Clark was with her. "For some mysterious reason you cut a wide swath wherever you go. The people in Valentine have probably opened a Clark Brennan Fan Club and it looks as if one is forming in this restaurant."

She hated to admit that she understood the appeal all too well. He may have been an irritant at first, but the same force of personality that propelled him into TV stardom, also served him well in a one-to-one setting. He had a winning combination of warmth and wit underscored by an appearance of total interest in the other person—whether it be her or Sally or one of the domino players in Neumann's Grocery.

"You cut something of a swath yourself." Clark nodded toward a table of four men in the corner. "Those guys, for instance, would be over making moves on you if I stepped away for even a minute."

"You exaggerate," she protested, yet that didn't stop her eyes from wandering in the direction he'd indicated.

"Not at all. Do you want to bet on it? I can slip off toward the men's room or make a telephone call and we'll find out. Of course, I already know what'll happen. You're a beautiful woman and those four are interested. They're thinking I'm one lucky son of a gun."

Jan felt her coloring heightening at the compliment, exaggerated and insincere though it might be. "Are we also going to bet on how many women accost you while you're out of my sight?"

"Oh, no. Besides, you're already convinced the women would make a move on me. Let's keep our wager simple. Five dollars on the blond guy in the gray suit coming over?" He started to get up.

When the man in question gave Jan a friendly nod, she knew this silly give-and-take had to end. She grabbed Clark's arm and he sat back down.

"So you see I was right?" Clark said, taking her hand between his own in a possessive gesture.

Jan pulled her hand away and reached for the glass of tea. She needed something cool. "So we both get a touch of interest now and then," she eventually managed to say. "Except you manage more than a touch. Valentine's adopted you as its own personal celebrity. And now that you're a property owner, you'll probably be elected mayor."

"I think 'celebrity' is the key word. With me out of television, interest will begin to wane. And after Garrett finishes trashing me all over town, my popularity will have the staying power of a Roman candle. I'll probably become the local pariah instead."

"Garrett's not usually one to run down people in public." That much was true and Jan felt obliged to defend her friend, even though in this case, she wondered if she was justified. Garrett had abandoned his usual discretion where Clark was concerned, sometimes ventilating to everyone within hearing distance.

"For me he might be willing to make an exception." Clark gave a sardonic laugh.

Jan sighed. What could she say? The chasm between the two men seemed to be widening before her eyes. Before she could dwell on it though, the waitress returned to take food orders.

"Have you given any more thought to B.J.'s train?" Clark asked, changing the subject. "I want to buy a gift for him and that's about the only thing he doesn't seem to have. Garrett's really been generous. His room looks like a toy store."

"Is that all due to Garrett?"

"I've sent him a few toys and souvenirs. A father's *supposed* to do that. My presents can't compare to what Garrett's bought."

There was no disguising Clark's resentment. "His grandfather does tend to overdo it," she agreed, "but he's been scaling back lately." Jan didn't add that it had been with her encouragement. "Aunt Sally says he was pretty indulgent with Toni, too."

Clark shook his head sadly. "That was a problem for us—she was used to getting everything she wanted and expected me to continue in her father's tradition."

"Was that what broke you up?"

"One of the things. But to be honest, there were plenty of other contributing factors—and Toni wasn't the only one at fault."

"Do you want to tell me about it?" Clark's comment gave him a boost in Jan's esteem department, especially since he wasn't taking the position of so many divorced men—placing all blame on their ex-wives. She wanted to hear more.

"Only if you'll reciprocate," he said cagily. "I'll tell you about my marriage, if you'll talk about yours."

The waitress spared Jan an answer by bringing their lunches. Using napkins as hot pads, she gingerly set two "specials"—cheese enchiladas with rice and refried beans—in front of them. Steam rose from the plates.

They ate silently for a few moments, Jan not wanting to reopen the marriage discussion. "Let's get back to B.J.," she said. "I'm sure he'll like the train. It'll remind him of the whistle of the Missouri-Pacific that passes by at bedtime."

"I thought it might generate some conversation between us," Clark said. "I can tell him about railroads in Europe—the excitement of the stations, the people, the scenery whizzing by. There's just something about traveling by rail. I'm hoping to show it to him sometime."

"Does that mean you're going back?"

"Only if I have my son with me."

The determination in his voice caused a shiver of dread to pass through Jan. She'd worried about this possibility before and apparently her concerns were warranted. Was this Clark's goal? Once he'd thwarted Garrett's attempts at custody, did he plan to take B.J. away? That would be the worst thing that could happen. For Garrett to lose his grandson after losing Toni would break his heart—and it wouldn't help Jan's emotional state, either.

"If I bought just the engine and caboose," Clark said, unaware that her mind has branched off in other directions, "then B.J. could help pick out the rest. Is that a good idea?"

It appeared that Clark knew more about young boys than she had realized. "He'd like that," she answered. "You two could come to the mall for an addition every so often. That'll keep the newness, plus give him an outing away from the ranch."

She paused to butter and fold a corn tortilla. "Occasionally—like today—Garrett interrupts lessons to take him somewhere. He studies better afterward. I think he sometimes gets bored at the Lazy M without other children his age."

"Yeah, I haven't noticed too many around. That's unusual, considering the number of hands working there."

"Most of the men who actually live on the ranch are single. The foreman has three boys, but they're older than B.J. and are tied up most of the time with school activities and sports. B.J.'s not a part of all that."

"Maybe he needs to be," Clark said. He put down his fork and leaned back in the booth. "Do you think home school is best for B.J., or should he be in a regular classroom?''

Jan looked at him quizzically. ''Are you trying to get me fired?'' Actually, she'd been planning on recommending that Garrett enroll his grandson in the local school next fall, when the new year began. Was Clark contemplating a transfer before then?

''No, I'm not trying to get you fired,'' he answered. ''Don't get all het up again. I wasn't disparaging your abilities. From everything I've seen you're a great teacher. But you just said he needs playmates.''

''True enough,'' Jan said. ''Except I'm not sure that now's a good time to make more changes in his life.''

''Things can't stay as they are.''

''No.'' Jan doubled her napkin and laid it on the table beside her, staying silent while Clark quickly surveyed the bill and handed the waitress a credit card. As they left the table, Jan continued. ''I realize B.J.'s future is uncertain. Unfortunately, so does he. Surely you and Garrett can keep that in mind and be a bit more tolerant of each other as you plot that future.''

''Tolerance isn't one of Garrett Montgomery's long suits.''

''Is it one of yours?'' she snapped back.

Clark held up a hand. ''Help! There was enough fire in that meal without more heat from you. Forget Garrett and come back to the toy store with me.''

He reinforced his request by taking charge of her packages in much the same manner he'd done at Neumann's Grocery. Once an engine, caboose and several sections of track were selected and paid for, Clark walked her to her car.

The sky was overcast and a light drizzle had begun. "I don't think there's any danger of the weather getting real nasty right away, but you never can tell. I'll follow you home."

As soon as Clark was out of sight, Jan turned on the motor. They might have had a relatively pleasant lunch and put their heads together on a present for B.J., but he seemed to be taking over. All of a sudden, he was becoming even more bossy than usual.

She had no intention of waiting for him to trail home after her like some overzealous bodyguard. Especially when there was nothing to worry about. The cold front and anticipated snow wouldn't arrive for several hours, maybe longer. And even if a blizzard loomed on the horizon, she still wouldn't have waited for him. There definitely needed to be some distance between them.

She'd only driven a few miles when she saw his black Pontiac race past a cattle truck and whip in behind her. He'd caught up with her and she might as well accept it. There'd be no escaping now. She forced her attention from his reflection in the rearview mirror to the traffic ahead. The narrow farm-to-market road demanded her concentration.

But it was difficult to think about driving. She couldn't get her mind off Clark, or resist sneaking peeks in the mirror. Try as she might to feel the opposite, Jan had to acknowledge that she was drawn to him. He was beginning to monopolize her thoughts to the exclusion of Glen, who hadn't surfaced in days.

Until Clark had arrived, she'd done little else but pine away. Some women said that all it took to get over one man was another, but Jan had never believed that. Had she been deceiving herself? Had

Clark, such a pain most of the time, been the necessary medicine for her heartache?

As much as Jan hated to admit it, she'd enjoyed lunch—even when sparring with Clark. Actually, *enjoyed* might be too much of an understatement to describe her response to their time together, although she couldn't come up with a better description. She didn't even want to try. Other men had vied for her attention since the divorce. But none had been successful. Now, Clark, who stood for much of what she thought she hated, was causing her pulse to accelerate. This was preposterous... she should know better.

The drizzle had stopped. Jan switched off the windshield wipers and turned on the radio. She needed something besides men to think about—the national or local news—anything. She glanced over at her shopping bags, at the one holding her present for B.J.

She'd come to love the boy almost as if he were her own. Unrealistic feelings, of course, because she had no claim of any kind on him. *Except the claim the heart makes*. Jan suddenly felt frightened. She'd vowed never to risk falling in love again. But she'd applied the oath only to a grown man and she'd let down her defenses with a small child. Now she faced the possibility of loss again—of losing B.J. What would she do then?

Even if Clark stayed in the area, clearly her relationship with his son would change. Even if she tried to maintain a friendship with Clark, there was no guarantee that he'd continue to give her access to B.J.

He might not be questioning her competency as a teacher, but it was hard to put aside that impression. He opposed continued tutoring and once the opportunity presented itself, he'd probably have B.J. enrolled in the local school. The idea troubled her.

Earlier today she felt sorry for Clark—sympathetic at his failed marriage, at his having to take a back seat to Garrett for B.J.'s affections. But the more she reflected on his actions, the more leery she became, suspicious that he'd been using some of his fabled charms on her.

For a father so new to the scene, there was almost too much display of parental concern—almost as if he was showboating. *Is Clark serious, or is he faking the solicitous daddy routine to get on my good side, to somehow win my support against Garrett*? And, if he wanted to get on her good side, why had he mentioned ending her role as B.J.'s instructor? The more Jan thought about the day, the more befuddled she became.

By the time she pulled into the drive at Sally's, she'd managed to work herself into what her aunt would describe as a full-blown "hissy fit," with Clark the obvious target, especially since he'd been right on her bumper the whole trip. "Why are you following me like some second-rate private detective?" she demanded as he drove up behind and got out of his car.

He looked puzzled. "What happened between Temple and here that got you all bent out of shape?"

Somehow his words only agitated her further. "Your trailing after me for one thing. For another, your—"

Clark's hands on her shoulders stopped Jan in midsentence. She gazed up at him, suddenly breathless by the look in his eyes.

"It appears that there's only one way to shut you up," he said, "and this is the way 'second-rate private detectives' do it." He pulled her toward him and his soft, firm lips met hers. For moments Jan resisted, trying to struggle out of his embrace. But her efforts were futile, his strong arms refusing to loosen their hold on her, her small frame powerless against his.

Then she could resist no longer and she melted into his kiss. It felt so good to have a man's arms around her again. Especially Clark's. She loved the press of his fit body and the wonderfully pungent smell of his woodsy after-shave.

Emotions Jan had thought she'd shuttered forever came bursting free. She tangled her fingers in his hair and nestled her body into his. She could grow to crave this. To crave this a lot. *And then what*? an inner voice asked.

Jan surfaced from the depths of passion as quickly as a deep-sea diver rising too fast from the ocean floor. And, much like the diver getting the bends, the action caused her whole body to ache. What in the world was she thinking of to allow him to touch her this way? With all her might, she shoved Clark away, bringing her hand up and slapping him soundly. "You're out of line, mister."

Clark stepped back, stunned at her rejection as he rubbed his reddened cheek and stared at her. For long moments, he was speechless. "I'll see you tomorrow," he finally said in a somber voice, still rubbing his cheek in bewilderment as he climbed into his car and drove away.

Jan stood fixed, as shocked as Clark about the slap. *What in heaven's name had come over her to act like that*? A tear rolled down her cheek. Then another. She was mortified by her behavior. Within a five-minute span, Jan had broken two rules—she'd let herself fall prey to a manipulative male and used physical abuse against another person. Never in her whole life had she struck anyone. Physical violence was abhorrent to her. Now, she'd not only offended her own sensibilities but she'd done so at the worst possible moment—in broad daylight where any and everyone could see. Sally's neighbors were probably peeking through the curtains right now—if they hadn't already rushed off to the telephone to share this juicy tidbit.

And they wouldn't just be describing the slap. Jan groaned. They'd also be prattling on about that kiss, a kiss meant for a bedroom in the dark of night, not the front yard in the middle of the afternoon. How would she ever explain to Sally—and to Garrett? She didn't even understand herself. Wiping away the tears, Jan opened the car trunk and took her parcels inside.

CHAPTER EIGHT

It was nearly dusk, the bare trees silhouetted against the strip of orange that outlined the horizon when Jan went to bed. A note to Sally saying that she had a sick headache was stuck to the refrigerator with a magnet. *It's a white lie*, Jan admitted, but justifiable under the circumstances. She couldn't abide a conversation with anyone right now, not even her beloved aunt.

Not that Sally would fault her if Jan confessed all the details of her unconscionable behavior this afternoon. Without a doubt, her aunt would be as empathetic as usual. But Jan was too dazed and distressed to discuss it at the moment. Surprisingly, the only person she would have even considered talking to was Clark.

She'd hoped he'd call so she'd have a chance to tell him how wretched she felt for her loss of control. But the telephone hadn't rung a single time and she didn't have the nerve to call him. Obviously she'd succeeded all too well in getting across the message that he was to leave her alone. Ever since he'd arrived in Valentine, she'd been telling herself that was what she wanted. So what was making her so miserable?

"It was the slap." Jan smoothed out her scrunched-up pillow and lay on her back, hazel eyes staring at the ceiling. How she wished the incident had never happened. She longed to have those minutes back to live all over again, or at least to obliterate them from her memory, to erase them as one did the dated messages on an answering machine.

But Jan admitted that it wasn't *only* the slap that bothered her—it was the kiss, too. Her cheeks heated when she thought of how she'd melted in Clark's arms. Her passion—frozen as the tundra since Glen's deception and desertion—had shot from subzero to the top of a thermometer during those moments in Clark's arms.

Jan heard Sally come in, putter around the kitchen, then tiptoe to her bedroom door and open it a crack. She feigned sleep until she heard Sally quietly close it again. Jan felt guilty about the pretense, but it was definitely the best thing for her to do tonight. She needed more time before facing her aunt, before seeking her counsel.

The house was silent when Jan padded down the hall to the kitchen the next morning for coffee. It was early, only six a.m., but Sally had already left for the post office as she would most days now, until the holiday rush was over.

Jan pulled back the curtains to check the weather. Sure enough, the morning sky was hidden behind a thick cloud cover. A winter storm was finally in the works.

Last week she'd wished in vain for inclement weather to protect her from Clark. Today, though, Jan wanted to see him, grovel a little, and get her apology over with. A night of tossing and turning, doing more fretting than sleeping, had convinced her that that was her best course of action.

Wispy snowflakes splattered against the windshield as Jan drove northward toward Garrett's ranch. She eyed the flakes warily, wondering whether she'd made a mistake in coming. A look at the fields passing by told her, however, that the ground was warm enough for the precipitation to melt almost as quickly as it hit. With luck, she'd have time to see Clark, get in her tutoring and be back home before driving became difficult.

The decision to keep going no more than made, she rounded a curve and the Mitsubishi skidded. Jan managed to keep the car from sliding off the shoulder and into a ditch, but the near-miss worried her. Perhaps she had been too optimistic; the weather seemed to be worsening rapidly, the temperature falling. Even with her coat and gloves, she felt chilled and she turned the heater up another notch.

Her hands gripped the steering wheel tightly as she cautiously navigated the now-glazing highway. Snow might occur seldomly in central Texas, but when it did, roads became obstacle courses and drivers were advised to stay home. Accumulations of the white stuff occurred too infrequently to justify the purchase and maintenance of expensive snow-clearing machines. *What condition are these roads going to be in by noon*?

"Just what I need—to be stranded at the Montgomery ranch," she grumbled aloud. Momentarily she considered turning back and phoning to say she wouldn't be out today, but she was much closer to the Lazy M than she was to town. Besides, B.J. had already missed one session this week. He would be disappointed if she didn't come. Most important, she needed to get that conversation with Clark out of the way.

Even though Jan was trying to maintain a stiff upper lip, now that the time was approaching, she dreaded facing him again. The words of penitence could be spoken, then filed away in the recesses of her brain to be quickly forgotten. But the memory of the kiss would remain there. She needed to banish the feelings Clark had aroused, but how could she as long as she worked at the ranch and had him around as a constant reminder?

She turned on the radio, twisting the dial in search of a weather report. At each setting, she got the same thing—a sampling of either George Strait, Garth Brooks or Reba McEntire, in mid-song. That wasn't surprising—most of the stations whose frequencies reached Valentine favored country and western performers, but couldn't one of the disk jockeys stop the music long enough to provide updates about winter storm warnings?

Finally Jan settled into one spot of the dial, determined to relax with the songs until she could get some information. The Judds were singing "Love Can Build A Bridge" and Jan started humming along, wishing Clark and Garrett could listen to the words and take them to heart.

At first, she had missed being able to tune in the classical and jazz sounds she'd listened to in California. Yielding to the fact there were none to be had in these parts, she'd had to choose between Country and Western or silence, and she'd grudgingly chosen the former. In a matter of weeks, however, she'd begun to develop a taste for the twangy voices and the plaintive lyrics. Now, she appreciated how the songs were like everyday life—the ups and downs, the happy and sad times. That was likely why Country and Western—once confined primarily to the American south and southwest—had attracted a worldwide audience.

It'd certainly be the music of choice at Garrett's Valentine's Day bash. It occurred to her that the party was only a week and a half away. Would Clark still be around? She'd wondered before and hoped each time to be rid of him by then. Now she knew that wasn't likely to happen, at least not by the fourteenth. Even a move from the Lazy M over to Zeke Phillips' place would make little difference. He'd still be only a few miles down the road. Feeling the way she did this morning, she'd need a few *million* miles to be free of his pull.

By the time Jan parked in front of the ranch house, the snowflakes had gotten larger and more numerous. A few clung to her black wool coat as she walked from the car to the porch, their intricate patterns visible for a few moments before the crystals melted away. Maybe B.J. would like to make paper snowflakes today, Jan thought as she tapped the knocker.

She was surprised when Rue Nell opened the door. Usually it was Garrett or B.J. or Clark. Today, she'd been hoping for Clark so she could quickly put the unpleasant task behind her. "Where is everybody?" she asked the cook.

"Mr. M. set out for Austin early this morning and the youngun's finishing his oatmeal." No details were provided on the reason for Garrett's trip, but Jan surmised that he was consulting another lawyer.

"What about Mr. Brennan?" Rue Nell hadn't mentioned Clark and Jan hesitated even to ask about him, but she had no choice. She had to get their talk out of the way so she could concentrate on her teaching.

"I was making beds last time I saw him. He was in his room pounding on that computer."

Computer? Jan hadn't thought about Clark bringing his work along and the idea bothered her. Was he filing a story from here? she wondered. Couldn't he cease being Mr. "All-Fired Important Reporter" for even a few weeks? She stopped herself. What was really upsetting her? The fact that rather than actually working, Clark might now be dodging her?

If he was hiding out, she didn't have to speculate as to the reason—it was anger over what happened yesterday. Or could there be a chance he was feeling as nonplussed over the kiss as she? Jan discounted that rationale. Clark had known too many women, was too cocksure and confident around females to let a little kiss bother him. He probably just wanted nothing more to do with a crazy woman. She decided to leave him alone for now.

Lessons were over and arts and crafts begun when Jan glanced out the schoolroom window, checking the weather for the umpteenth time that morning. The snow was as thick as goose down feathers in a go-for-broke pillow fight and it'd been that way for the last two hours. She shivered as she surveyed the landscape and left B.J. taping up snowflake cutouts as she headed to the kitchen. They both needed something warm to drink.

While Rue Nell was vacuuming the rooms upstairs, Jan started a fresh pot of coffee. Why did Garrett have to run off today of all days? She'd be a lot more comfortable if he were around. Besides, it worried her that he'd chosen to tackle the highway when weather conditions were worsening.

She glanced at her watch. Surely he was already in Austin, or at least close, and would remain overnight. Despite the fact he was a skilled driver and that his huge Chrysler Imperial gave added protection, there was no reason for him to take chances.

Her worries about Garrett's welfare aside, she needed to decide her own course of action. Should she start for home or stay at the ranch? Common sense said that staying put was the safest route to take. This downfall wasn't going to let up anytime soon and it only took a flashback to the spin this morning, plus a glance out the window at the white-blanketed lawn to tell her the roads had become treacherous.

"You're still here?" Clark's voice startled her.

"Not for long," she answered, switching on the kettle to boil water for B.J.'s instant hot chocolate. She took a moment to turn around, in her mind composing what to say before facing Clark. The minute she saw him though, Jan promptly forgot her pledge to make amends. There was a look in his eyes, not exactly a smirk, but close. A look that said, "Ready for Round Two?" Once she'd seen him, self-consciousness warming her face and neck, her choice was made. Driving back to Sally's now seemed the less risky alternative.

Snow in these parts usually disappeared as fast as it fell, but there was always the chance it might stay on the ground for days. From the looks of things, that could easily happen this time. Jan had no intention of being isolated with Clark for a single night, much less several.

"You're not going anywhere," Clark said. "Even to consider leaving is crazy. That car of yours would be sliding all over the place before you got a mile down the road."

"You're probably right," she said, deciding to play it cool. "No big deal though. I'll ask one of the hands to take me home. The ranch has a couple of four-wheel drive vehicles." She picked up the kitchen telephone to ring the bunk house. There was no answer.

"Every man on the place is out," he said.

"So I'll just hang around until they get back." She removed a mug from the cabinet and filled it with coffee, then hopped up on the counter.

"You may have a long wait. They're tending to all the horses and livestock. It could be hours before anyone's free. By then they'll be so dog-tired, they'll probably head directly home or to the bunk house to collapse."

She made no response, but sipped her coffee with pretended indifference, as uncomfortable as ever in Clark's presence.

Clark got himself a cup of coffee and sat down at the table, stretching his long legs in front of him. He brought the coffee to his lips. "Hmm, this hits the spot. I'd forgotten that Texas can get so cold. What's my boy up to?"

"Finished with his lessons and making snowflakes and valentines. I'd better go tell him goodbye. I think I'll try to drive after all." She jumped down from her countertop perch.

"Have you got some kind of death wish? It's not safe out there." He stood up, towering over her.

"I can handle it. I've driven in snow before." She got another mug down and started making B.J.'s chocolate.

"This isn't just snow." He took her by the shoulders and turned her around to face him. "It's sleet, too. You know *sleet*—that icy stuff that turns the roads into skating rinks?"

Jan tried to shrug out of his grasp, but Clark held her fast. "Now be honest, would you leave if Garrett were here?"

Of course, Jan wanted to say. But Clark knew better. "Probably not," she answered, wondering if the admission would bring a cutting comment from Clark. She remembered all too well his charge that there could be something less than proper about her staying overnight at the ranch. But it seemed that Clark had forgotten his accusation.

"Then it's obvious you're refusing to stay because of me, because of what happened yesterday afternoon."

"That's . . . that's nonsense," she stammered.

"I don't think so."

"Oh, all right," she conceded reluctantly. "That's exactly the reason. I'm sorry and ashamed. I don't know what got into me. I've never slapped a man before in my life. Even my ex-husband, and if anyone had it coming, he did."

"Don't try to change the subject to your ex. Anyway, forget the slap. I wasn't upset."

"You weren't? Honestly?"

"Honestly. I was a little startled, but after thinking about it, I believe I understand."

He twisted a strand of her glossy brown hair around his finger. "I liked kissing you, Jan. In fact, the more

I thought about it, the more I could hardly wait for it to happen again." From his expression, he was ready to pull her to his lips right then.

"It's not going to happen again," she said, wishing she wasn't trapped between him and the counter.

"Oh, no?" His thick eyebrows raised. "Why not?"

"Just because, that's why." Her voice was unsteady. "I don't want to discuss this."

"You seem to have a laundry list of things you don't want to discuss, but whether you want to talk about it or not, that kiss isn't going away." He stepped back and picked up his coffee mug, taking a swallow. "But I realize from your reference to your ex-husband that the timing was wrong—it happened too soon for you."

"What do you mean by 'too soon'?"

"Before you've had opportunity enough to work through all your feelings about your marriage, your resentment toward men in general. One day you'll be ready, and—"

"Never." His comments stung. "Not with you. *Especially* not with you. In fact, it's become crystal clear to me that my staying here tonight won't work. I'm going home. Take B.J. his chocolate." She slammed the cup on the countertop, causing a pool of chocolate to slosh out, and started toward the front door.

"You're about as mule-headed as they come," Clark called out as he followed her through the house. "I don't have time to argue with you now though." He grabbed her purse off the entry hall table and fished out the car keys, depositing them in the pocket of his jeans. "Just so I don't have to worry about you doing something stupid behind my back."

She started to grab for the keys, but stopped. As tight as his jeans were, there was no way she'd go searching around in one of the pockets. "You can't keep me a prisoner," she said adamantly.

He just grinned in response and began easing into the new sheepskin jacket, thick enough to ward off even today's frigid cold. "I need to help the men with the stock. *You* take B.J. the chocolate, and when he finishes, tell him to bundle up and move those kittens to the kitchen. They're too young to stay in the barn in this weather." He grabbed his new Stetson from a deer antlers hat rack, yanked it down over his brow and disappeared outside.

She felt like running after him and flinging her cup or something equally injurious at his departing back. This was too much. Why did Clark have some mystical power to make her lose her temper? It wasn't the car keys—she had an emergency set concealed in her rear bumper—but the fact that every word he said nettled her and that his domineering actions caused her to react in ways she'd never considered before. Not even with Glen. The locals would say Clark was a burr under her saddle. That was putting it mildly. She just didn't know what to do about it.

Despite her declaration about leaving, Jan knew it would be foolhardy to try to get home. The wind was whipping the snow into deep drifts. Clark's hat had blown off twice while she was watching him through the windows. She was marooned here and she knew it.

Nevertheless, one thing was certain. If she was going to have to put up with Clark's company, then she couldn't foam at the mouth every time he spoke, and she certainly couldn't start throwing crockery. She had to think of B.J. *Speaking of B.J.* She backtracked to get his hot chocolate, then set off to the schoolroom to tell him about the cats. Between the two of them, they could probably transfer the animals to the house in one trip.

Garrett phoned at three to advise that, yes, he was remaining in Austin. Then Jan called Sally and told her not to expect her back tonight. Her aunt sounded relieved, even though most of their conversation centered around the mail backlog rather than the unusual road conditions. Thank goodness Sally lived only a few blocks from her job, because Jan knew she'd never permit the weather to interfere with her official duties. "Neither rain, nor snow...." Wasn't that how it went? Her aunt was committed to the old postal service creed, especially when it concerned her favorite holiday.

With Jan's help, B.J. had brought the cats inside. Playing with the animals and his new train set, watching the near blizzard and finishing his valentines occupied his attention for most of the afternoon. He also kept a frequent check on the window, happily observing the snow as the accumulation continued.

When Clark reappeared with a red nose and chapped cheeks in late afternoon, the little boy begged to go outside and play. Clark told him no. "The weather's too bad right now. Besides, it's almost dark."

It wasn't the first time B.J. had asked to play outside. Jan had been putting him off all day, with one excuse after another. Now she wondered whether she should have made an exception and allowed him a short romp. But the wind chill was near zero and B.J. had been shivering just from the brief run to the stable to fetch the kittens.

"You and I will get out and build a snowman tomorrow," Clark promised.

"That sounds like a good idea," Jan chimed in, hoping to prevent an outburst. She might hate forcing herself to be agreeable around Clark, but she was determined to do it for B.J.'s sake. "It's supposed to clear up by then," she added.

"Okay." B.J. sounded unperturbed.

Jan was surprised. She'd expected at least an argument from the child, possibly even another fit. Instead, he had calmly accepted his father's refusal and gone back to playing contentedly with the kittens. Every time she was with them, Clark seemed to be getting better at handling his son, and B.J. seemed to be adjusting to the handling. At least when his grandfather wasn't around.

Upon completion of the ranch chores, the crew had scurried on home, Rue Nell included. She was married to Tom, one of the hands. They had a small house at the edge of the ranch and before long it, too, would be inaccessible.

All the staff who lived on the Lazy M spread were secure in their homes or bunk house quarters and Jan, Clark and B.J. were alone in the main house. After what had transpired that morning between Clark and her, Jan was even more unsettled about this arrangement. B.J., however, seemed adequate as a chaperon.

He and Clark worked on a Sesame Street jigsaw puzzle on the kitchen table while Jan made dinner. Rue Nell had left a cut-up chicken in the refrigerator, so Jan baked it along with some potatoes. Just the sort of hearty meal that would appeal to B.J., although he might not be too excited about the field greens salad she'd made in an attempt to bring some balance to their dinner. As they ate, the child monopolized the conversation.

"Speckles wanted to come in the house, too," he said, giggling. "What do you think Grandpa would say if we brought him in?"

"He'd probably order you and me out to the stables with Speckles," Clark said, and B.J. giggled even more.

Right now it was difficult for Jan to imagine that father and son had ever been alienated. She continued listening as they talked. In spite of her many reservations about Clark, she was pleased at how comfortable the boy had become with his father. The change was remarkable.

Clark insisted that he and B.J. clear the table and clean the kitchen, so Jan left them alone and went into the den to watch television. Later they joined her for a program and afterward returned to the puzzle. Jan was amazed how the presence of a child could diffuse the tension between two adults.

She stayed curled on the couch, snuggled comfortably under a soft crocheted afghan. For a couple of hours she watched a series of situation comedies, eventually becoming drowsy. A creak of the stairs told her Clark and B.J. were going up to bed and she wanted to follow suit, but was determined to stay awake to check the late news. She was hoping against hope for the promise of an immediate warming front.

Clark joined her just as the news came on, making Jan regret that she hadn't escaped to her room when she had the opportunity. The bottle of wine and two stemmed glasses which he set on the coffee table in front of her told her that he hadn't popped in just to bid her good-night. Neither spoke, but she sat up when it became obvious he intended to sit beside her on the couch.

The lead news story was today's weather and it was worse than Jan had thought—Texas was snowed in from Amarillo to Austin with flurries as far south as San Antonio and Houston. The newscaster reported that citrus growers in the valley which bordered Mexico were worried about their crops, afraid that a hard freeze might damage the orange and grapefruit trees.

Clark handed over a glass of wine—a rich, red claret, then picked up the television remote control and lowered the volume. He turned toward her, resting an arm on the back of the sofa.

Jan pushed the afghan between them and picked up a throw pillow, surreptitiously, she thought, easing it between them, also.

Clark laughed. "Are you attempting to erect a barrier?"

The fact that he'd seen right through her was irritating. She set her wine down, untouched. "It's late and I'm tired. If you came to pick a fight—no thanks. If you were planning a romantic rendezvous instead, I'm sorry to disappoint you, but count me out."

In answer he grabbed the pillow and afghan and tossed them on the floor, but made no attempt to move closer to her. Yet somehow she knew that if she tried to leave, he'd stop her. That would mean he'd touch her, something she couldn't allow to happen. Not with her low resistance to his physical charms.

He handed the glass back to her. "Drink your wine, Jan. It'll relax you."

"I don't need to relax."

He chuckled ruefully. "Don't you? I'd say—using the Valentine vernacular—that you're as nervous as a long-tailed cat in a roomful of rocking chairs." He took a sip of wine. "You want nothing more than to run up those stairs and hide in your room, bolting the door against me and the rest of the world."

"Do you see me running or hiding?"

He laughed again. "Isn't that why you're here in Valentine? But you can't hide from life, you know. Not for long, anyway. Wherever you are, it has a way of catching up with you."

CHAPTER NINE

"YOU'RE speaking from experience, of course."

"Are you sure you don't want to fight, Jan?" He leaned closer to her, causing her to press back further into the corner of the sofa. She remembered all too well what had happened the last time she'd quarreled with him and that was in late afternoon, with the specter of a daytime viewing audience watching from nearby windows. To squelch any arguing, he'd planted a kiss on her that had coursed all the way to her toes.

Now they were alone. The wine, the glowing embers of the hearth—this was entirely too cozy. Who knew what kind of peacemaking strategy he might employ this time? She unfolded her legs and stood up.

"It's been a long day and I'm going to bed." Observing his slight grin, she added, "Alone."

"Were you suggesting that I was planning to join you? Or to lure you into *my* bed?"

"I wasn't suggesting anything. Good night." She was halfway up the stairs when she heard his soft, mocking, "Sleep well, Jan." Without responding, she hastened to her room.

Undressing for bed Jan thought how strange it felt being alone in the house with Clark and B.J. She'd never given a moment's consideration about whether she should stay here when Garrett was home. And still wouldn't, she realized. Whatever Clark had implied.

Those other times, she'd stayed simply because the child wanted her to, or because she was joining him and Garrett on a trip to some attraction in San Antonio. She even kept a change of clothing and a nightshirt here for just such occasions.

But to stay now...this was different. Clark's presence changed everything. No matter how much she tried, Jan couldn't put his embrace, or that searing kiss, out of her mind. Obviously, Clark hadn't forgotten, either.

According to the television report, the chilly temperatures would keep the roads clogged for several days—days she was going to be isolated with Clark Brennan. *Thank heavens for B.J.* Perhaps his company would keep the two supposedly mature adults from losing their heads and doing something they might later regret.

The snow lay in deep mounds the next morning, but as predicted, the skies were clearing, the cloud cover not as pervasive. Although early, the Lazy M had already come to life. From the window, Jan could see Clark and B.J. tromping a path across the yard, headed in the direction of the barn. Cowhands labored in the corral, pitching out hay for the penned-up stock. Others were astride their horses, plodding through the snowbanks to tend cattle in the far pastures. She padded to the adjacent bathroom to dress. A hot shower would invigorate her and warm her, as well. In view of all the activity, she needed to get going before accusations rose about her being a slugabed.

Fresh-brewed coffee waited in the kitchen. Jan leisurely drank a cup and breakfasted on whole-wheat toast while watching the morning news on the small countertop TV. Calico, the mother cat, curled around Jan's ankles and Jan reached down to scratch behind the animal's ears. A plaintive purr told her that hunger was motivating Calico's affection and, as bidden, she filled the cat's bowl with dry food from a sack in the pantry. The two of them, Jan and Calico, had just finished eating when B.J. came in, cheeks aflame from the cold and eyes bright with happiness.

"Hi, Jan." He sidled over to the box in the corner and tenderly petted Calico and her babies. Jan heard a couple of tiny mews.

"If we hurry with school, we can be done by the time the chores are over. Can we hurry?" He stood in front of her, digging his toe into the pattern of the vinyl floor, anticipation on his face as he waited for her answer.

"Of course we can." She gently fluffed his hair. "Do you want something to eat or drink before we get started?"

"No, thank you," he answered, already halfway down the hall.

Jan made every effort to keep their classes interesting that morning. She wanted B.J.'s attention to be here in the schoolroom, rather than outside. But she needn't have worried. He was unusually cooperative, eager to finish one assignment and move on to the next. By midmorning, all her lesson plans had been completed.

"Enough for today," she announced. "Go find your father and tell him you're ready to build that snowman." B.J. needed no more prompting. As he scampered off in search of Clark, she smiled. Snow was too special in this part of Texas for a child to miss the fun of it. Or an adult, either, she decided.

Living in Southern California as she had for the last few years, meant that she hadn't seen—much less built—a snowman in a long time.

Too bad she couldn't take advantage of the opportunity. She'd come dressed for warmth yesterday—her long reefer coat, wool beret and leather gloves were fine for getting about in a car, but hardly practical for romping in the snow. Instead she'd bake some chocolate-chip cookies as a treat for B.J.

But Clark wouldn't hear of that. "You're being chicken—afraid of the snowball fight we've scheduled."

"I'm more afraid of freezing to death."

"Then we'll have to see that doesn't happen."

Within the hour, Jan was properly attired for the outdoors in a layered assortment of borrowed clothes. One of the ranch hands had donated thermal underwear, Clark had provided a second pair of socks, some of Garrett's work gloves covered her own leather ones, and Rue Nell had rummaged up a ski jacket. Jan couldn't help but be excited. She was as anxious as B.J. to seize the moment.

Ranch work was suspended as cowhands joined Jan, Clark, B.J. and the foreman's children—two teenagers and an eleven-year-old who'd been released from school—first in a free-for-all snowball fight and then ceasing combat to create an entire snow family. Once the mother, father, boy, girl and a lopsided dog were constructed, the group scoured the grounds gathering materials for eyes and noses. Jan begged off. "My gloves are wet and my hands are freezing. I'm going in."

She hadn't expected Clark to follow after her and was unprepared for the stomping of his boots behind her on the porch. He then bent down to help her remove hers. "These are soaked all the way down to your socks." He peeled off the layers and began massaging her bare foot. When Jan jerked the foot back, he reached for the other one, once again removing the boot and socks, once again massaging her reddened toes.

Jan felt goose bumps on her skin, not from the frosty temperatures, but in response to his touch. She started to pull away, but he loosened his grip and stood, picking her up and carrying her inside.

"This isn't necessary," she complained, hearing the chuckles from the rest of the group, who'd momentarily abandoned their play to watch the dynamics between the couple.

"But it's fun, isn't it," he said, ignoring their audience and pushing the door closed behind them. He smiled and let her body slide slowly down his, until her feet met the floor.

For long moments Jan stood there, entrapped by the irresistible blue eyes that held her motionless. She felt certain he would try to kiss her. And she wanted him to, even though the thought frightened her. An inner voice told her to flee while there was still time, yet her body refused to respond to any warnings, and she remained incapable of severing the connection.

It was Clark who broke the spell, conscious no doubt that B.J. could burst in at any moment. "You'd better get something on those feet before you catch cold, and I'd better get out of these boots and mop up the mess I've made before Rue Nell shows up and takes a broom after me."

Jan headed upstairs, her mind spinning. Was she imagining that Clark's voice sounded huskier, more sensual? Had their moment of tender awareness affected him, too?

It was better not to think about it, she concluded as she went in search of dry clothing. She changed into sweats and went to borrow another pair of dry socks from Clark.

She could hear him moving about in his bedroom and she knocked on his door. He was tucking a plaid flannel shirt into a fresh pair of jeans when he eventually answered. Jan pointed at her bare feet and he went over to the bureau.

"Here. Take your pick—argyles or white crew socks?"

She chose the white ones. "Thanks. You're a lifesaver."

"Jan?"

"Yes?"

"I... that is, will you promise me something?"

She looked at him apprehensively.

"Don't look so scared. It's really not such a difficult something. All I'm asking is that you overlook the past and move forward. Can you do that? Can you quit second-guessing my motives and let us become friends?"

Jan knew that she wanted to. Everything between them seemed to have changed. "I can try," she answered simply.

"That's enough for now." He tossed the argyle socks back into the drawer. "Are you ready for some lunch?"

"I'll be down in a minute."

Jan dallied in her room, rubbing her still-red feet with aloe vera lotion before putting on Clark's socks. Once she was alone, all her doubts and fears seemed to resurface. The way she continued to react erratically to him was becoming ridiculous. No one understood that better than she. And she wasn't proud of herself. A few moments before he could have gotten her to agree to almost anything. This had to stop. Clark was just a man—no different from Glen or other men, the majority of them worthless to the core. But even as the thought passed through her mind, Jan knew it wasn't true.

First, most men weren't as shallow as Glen and she was being unfair attributing his shortcomings to the entire gender. Second, Clark was unlike any man she'd ever met. Critical yet affectionate, fun-loving yet solid, world-traveled yet tied to his Texas roots. Whatever his problems with Garrett, whatever his motives for staying away from B.J., he was one of a kind. *Stupid, you're just being taken in again*, that foreboding voice whispered in her head. Jan realized sadly that she might never again be able to trust sufficiently to wipe such messages from her brain.

But it wasn't her distrust that caused her to be so unsettled right now. It was the confinement, the forced familiarity. Even a silly trifle like wearing an article of his clothing—an article as impersonal as socks—seemed to promote another layer of closeness between her and Clark. She needed to calm down. The only route to serenity, however, would be distance, something that wasn't going to happen for a day or two. While Garrett's house was spacious, it seemed incredibly small to her now.

When Jan heard Clark's call, she reluctantly went back downstairs. If she hid in her room much longer, he'd seek her out, probably make fun of her cowardice.

She found him in the kitchen, an oven-mitted hand wrapped around the handle of a big cast-iron pot. "Chilli," he explained. "Rue Nell cooked it at her place and dropped it off." He set the pot on top of the stove. "B.J.'s eating with the other children. That is, if they're not outdoors again."

"I hope he doesn't catch cold. He—"

"Not to worry, little mother. He came by for some dry clothes. My son's a lot tougher than you think. I doubt we'll be able to persuade him to come in before dark. A snow fort is next on the agenda, I understand."

"Kids." Jan shook her head. She walked over to the range and took the lid off the chilli. A spicy aroma drifted up. Rue Nell's chilli was legendary around these parts and the perfect meal for a winter day. Apparently Clark had another female conquest in Garrett's cook.

It wasn't only Rue Nell though. All the ranch staff seemed to like Clark. He might have been unwelcome at first, but he'd obviously won them over. They'd been friendly and accepting today, talking and joking with him like he'd always been a part of the Lazy M. But then, their boss hadn't been around. Jan wondered if the playfulness they'd all enjoyed would have happened if Garrett were at home. She didn't want to think about that right now.

"Do you mind if we turn it on?" she asked Clark, motioning to the television as she arranged two place mats on the table.

"Of course not. But I'm beginning to think you're addicted to that thing." He reached over and pushed the power button. The noon news was just beginning.

Jan smiled guiltily. He was right, of course, it did seem that way. But she wasn't about to admit to using the set as a buffer from him in much the same fashion as she had the pillows on the couch.

While they ate, Jan and Clark listened to the details of the winter weather. During a commercial, she gazed at him and asked, "Do you miss it—television, I mean?"

"Do you?" he countered.

"I asked first," Jan said.

"So you did." He pushed his empty bowl aside. "I expected to." He sat thoughtfully, his elbows resting on the table, his palms cupping his chin. "Funny thing is...I don't. I guess I was getting burnt out and didn't realize it until I stopped to catch my breath." He shook his head and pointed toward the screen where a wind-whipped correspondent was struggling against a curtain of pelting sleet and snow to describe the multiple car accidents on Interstate 35. "I don't envy that guy one iota."

"But how long will those feelings last?" she asked. "How long before you're itching to get back in?" For some reason, Jan needed to know his answer. Did Clark plan on putting down stakes permanently, or was Valentine just a brief sojourn in his life? Part of her argued that she wanted to know for B.J.'s sake. Another part reluctantly acknowledged that she also wanted the answer for herself.

"The way I feel right now, there's no likelihood of that," Clark said. "I've seen enough pain, suffering and embattled countries to last a lifetime." His eyes seemed to glaze as he apparently relived some moment from his past.

Jan watched him sympathetically. "Why do I get the impression you're talking about a particular country? Was there an unsettling incident that caused you to return to the United States?"

He gazed out the window, still lost in thought. "Yeah," he finally said, "sort of." His attention returned to the room. "That and other things. I'll tell you about them sometime." He got up from his chair and carried his bowl and silverware to the sink.

Jan didn't prod further. Her question had obviously disconcerted Clark and dislodged unpleasant memories. Now she regretted bringing up the subject. "Are you going back outside?"

"I promised I would. How about you?"

"Oh, no. I've had enough for one day. Think I'll read awhile."

With the uninterrupted time, Jan quickly finished the novel she'd been carrying around in her briefcase, then curled up on the couch trying to nap. She dozed for a few moments, but noise from the front lawn kept rousing her. Finally curiosity got the best of her and she got up and looked out the window. A second snowball fight was in full swing, the youngsters and Clark lined up against the bunk house crew. Globs of snow were hurling through the air like soft, sloppy missiles.

Jan smiled. The once pristine white carpet was now interlaced with tracks, a few sprigs of brown grass visible where the cover had been removed to build the forts. She glanced at her watch and headed for the kitchen. Surely they couldn't stay out much longer.

Those cookies she'd planned earlier would be just the thing for an afternoon snack.

The first pan of cookies was being transferred to a plate when Clark entered through the back door. "Smells wonderful in here." He tossed his hat and gloves on the table, then poured a cup of coffee and took a couple of sips before removing his coat. "I'm too old to keep up with that gang, but I think they've finally run down." He snatched a cookie from the plate. "B.J.'s going to spend the night with the other boys."

Jan abruptly stopped spooning batter onto the baking sheet. She didn't like this one bit. Without B.J. here, she would be *totally* alone with Clark. Although she'd frequently bemoaned the boy's lack of playmates, tonight wasn't the time to rectify the problem. But what could she do or say to prevent it? How could she begrudge B.J. this opportunity to be with other children?

That would be Clark's response if she voiced her misgivings. No doubt he'd also remind her that, as the boy's father, permission for a sleep over was his prerogative. She'd just have to struggle through the evening as best she could.

"I put some steaks out earlier," he said, breaking into her thoughts. "I'll broil them whenever you're hungry."

"I can do it."

"I'm not hopeless in the cooking department," he told her. "We'll team up—you can bake potatoes and make the salad and I'll whip up my famous steak marinade. But first, I'm going to get out of these wet clothes." He grabbed his coffee and another cookie, then left.

* * *

Although distressed about their too cozy situation, Jan couldn't resist contemplating how companionably they worked preparing dinner. Glen had never lifted a finger with cooking or cleaning and when Garrett visited Sally, he was always content to be waited on. Her father, too, seemed to hold set ideas about what was "women's work." But Clark made no such distinctions. He didn't merely prepare and broil the steaks; he also cleaned up after himself and offered to chop vegetables for the salad.

They ate on TV trays in the den, once again watching the news. Despite being caught at it, Jan continued to use the television as a way to avoid closeness. After the meal was over, Clark carried their dishes to the kitchen.

Jan conceded that it had been one of the best days in her recent memory. Clark's earlier tag of "little mother" came to her mind. She knew he hadn't meant it literally; he was simply teasing her for being overprotective of B.J. But a couple of times she had fantasized about what it would be like to actually *be* the child's mother. Because she loved B.J., it was an appealing idea. Could it also be because it would serve as a permanent connection with his father?

"What drivel," she muttered to herself, picking up the remote and clicking through the channels. Surely there was something on that would capture her fancy. And Clark's, too, she hoped, seeing him re-enter the room. He carried a tray of coffee and brandy and sat down beside her.

Conversation was halted as they watched a nature documentary. When it ended, Clark switched off the set and rose to put music on Garrett's aging stereo console, some old Big Band records from the 1940s. He added several logs to the fire, then sat back down.

"You asked me earlier why I came back to the States," he said.

Jan nodded, both curious and grateful that he'd found something for them to talk about. A long evening lay ahead and talking was better than . . . than other things they could be doing.

"It seems as though most of my adult life has been devoted to reporting," he began. "First at the campus station, then for a few years I was one of the minions covering local news. When I transferred to New York my career took off. In the past few years, I've been on the scene at wars, famines, earthquakes, you name it. . . . At first it was exciting—a country boy from Texas traveling in the hot spots of the world. . . ." Clark rested his hands on his knees and stared down at the floor. Several minutes passed before he continued.

"Although the reporting eventually became routine, still there were moments of excitement. But I'd changed. Once I was shocked, sympathetic—later I became almost immune to the suffering I witnessed. You have to survive. Strange isn't it that most news is about people being *hurt* in some way or another? Anyway, my indifference came to a screeching stop recently."

He picked up the decanter of brandy, taking his time to fill two glasses, obviously mulling over just how much to tell her. "Do you remember seeing a story about that TV cameraman who was critically injured by sniper fire a month ago?"

Jan shook her head, suddenly realizing how isolated she'd allowed herself to become. She only vaguely remembered reading about a newsman being shot. "I don't watch much television anymore," she admitted. "Actually I've probably turned on a set more in the past two days than in the past two years."

Clark didn't question why, probably because he was too involved in his story. "Bill Barnes. I was standing about three feet away from him when it happened."

A chill ran through Jan as she comprehended that Clark could just as easily have been the victim. Had he been injured, also? There was no way for her to know without asking. "Were you hurt, too?"

"A few scratches from some shrapnel. Nothing serious, but it was a close call—for both of us." He handed one of the glasses of brandy to Jan.

"How did it happen?"

"Let's just say we were somewhere we shouldn't have been."

Jan knew there was a longer story waiting to be told and she was impatient to hear it all, but she wouldn't push. Clark was willing to talk and he would eventually answer all her questions. She would have to let him proceed at his own pace.

"Bill was a friend," Clark continued. "In fact we'd spent most of the last year together—so I went with him to London, to the hospital. We'd no sooner arrived than his family appeared—his wife, their two daughters. Suddenly I felt lonelier than I'd ever felt in my life. If the situation had been reversed, who would have come to me? I didn't know then about Toni's death, but I had no reason to think my ex-wife would have bothered.

"B.J. was too young to travel alone, of course—and anyway, like you've often reminded me, he was a virtual stranger. So that left a cousin—my only other family. We're fairly close, but unless I was mortally wounded, I doubt he would cross the Atlantic to sit at my bedside. It struck me loud and clear what I was missing. I needed more in my life than my career—I needed my son."

"And it took that incident to make you realize it?"

"No. Actually, it'd been growing inside me for some time. I just hadn't had an opportunity to do anything about it."

Clark picked up his glass of brandy and stared into the amber liquid. "I tried to call B.J. from England and was told Toni's phone had been disconnected, so I tried the ranch. Garrett simply said B.J. was asleep and he had no intention of waking him. I vowed then and there to make some changes—in my life and in my relationship with B.J." He turned the glass on end and drained the contents, then refilled it. "You were probably expecting something a lot more dramatic."

Actually, Jan hadn't known what to expect. "So you've returned and established a bond with B.J. You have someone to love you and care about you."

"I'm not so sure. I'm just taking one day at a time."

"But what about your work?"

"It's of little consequence now."

Jan was bewildered. His story was dramatic, sure, but not so earth-shattering as to make him give up reporting forever. "Don't you think that one day soon you'll want to be back in action?"

Clark shrugged. "The die is cast."

Jan wasn't so certain. Perhaps one event had shaken Clark and made him long for his own flesh and blood, for a home of his own, but it was an impulsive course of action, one that he might grow weary of. What would happen when Valentine became routine—would he just run off again?

"You're awfully quiet. Is there something else you want to know?"

"I suppose there is." If their relationship had any chance of progressing Jan needed at least one more answer. "You've told me why you came back, but why did you stay away so long?"

CHAPTER TEN

"I'VE tried to explain before," he said, exasperation showing in his voice.

"I know, and I wouldn't listen. I didn't know you as well then as I do now."

"Does that mean you're finally willing to hear what I have to say, to believe me?"

"Yes. Tell me, Clark."

He rubbed his jaw reflectively and Jan noticed that a faint stubble of whiskers was appearing on his smooth skin. "It just happened," he said. "I never expected to be out of the U.S.—to be gone from B.J.—that long." He pressed his fingers against his lips, bleak memories clouding his eyes.

Jan waited. Was that all he was going to say? "You told me earlier that you didn't want to pass B.J. back and forth every weekend," she prompted.

"That's right. I didn't want a schedule for him like some frantic European tour—but I've *always* wanted to be part of his life. I optimistically assumed it would be easy to accomplish, and I didn't foresee any complications even when Toni moved back to Texas. I figured I'd simply hop on a plane every few months, plus keep in touch by telephone and by mail. My work wouldn't interfere to any greater extent than when the two of them lived in New York. I could still send him trinkets and cards from the various countries I visited. Oh, I rationalized myself right through any concerns. Besides, I guess I felt guilty about Toni being stuck on the East Coast. I knew how much she missed home, even when we were married."

"But you didn't feel guilty enough to come back to Texas with her and try again." She wanted to be fair, but she also wanted the whole story, not some whitewashed version of what had happened.

"True enough. Like I said before, I take my share of the blame. Anyway..." he paused, "it wouldn't have mattered. Looking back, I can see how our marriage was destined for failure. We were just too different. Toni loved parties and night life and—"

"And you loved your job."

"That's right. I already know what's coming next—'Neither of you loved B.J. enough to work out those differences and stay together.' Is that about it?"

Even though he'd summed up her thoughts precisely, Jan hesitated. After all, marriages ended all the time, whether one wanted them to or not. Hers, for example. She could hardly afford to cast stones. "No matter what I may have thought, it's not my place to pass judgment. But explain to me about Garrett. Why has he been so adamant that you've ignored your son? What caused him to hold such an intractable position?"

"It's a natural tendency to take sides in a dispute—Toni was his daughter, his only child. But I can't deny that he's partly right. I found being a long-distance father a lot trickier than I thought it would be. Paying child support and making sure birthday and Christmas gifts arrived on time weren't enough. And seeing B.J. was a nightmare. Logistically and otherwise."

Clark picked up the coffee carafe and gestured toward Jan. She nodded and he poured their cups, once more buying time to gain an extra second for composing his answer. "At first, my trips to visit him came off just like I planned. But the settings were less than perfect. We'd see each other in a hotel room, at the zoo or an amusement park, or worse, at Toni's town house in Austin with her hovering over my shoulder. Our marriage was ending and the strain between us evident. A toddler can sense tension. B.J. became shy and awkward around me and I began to wonder whether I was doing him more harm than good by coming." He combed his fingers through his hair.

"So you just stopped? From what I've heard, it had been more than a year since you'd last had any personal contact."

"Nightmare visits or not, I would never have stopped. I was intent on keeping up the visits and biding my time until he was older. I hoped that once he could travel on his own, we'd be able to have more time together, eventually get relaxed with one another. Until that happened, I knew I had to be content with the infrequent trips and the tension."

"So what happened the past year that made you stay away?"

"There were extenuating circumstances," Clark said, in an echo of Sally MacGuire's earlier words.

"Like what?"

"I told you about Bill's injury. Immediately prior, the two of us had spent the year in a desolated area of central Africa. Few telephones around, to say the least, and the mail service atrocious. I sent letters, but I'm not sure how many got through.

"Anyway, suffice it to say I wasn't visiting one of the garden spots of the world. Numerous factions were struggling for control and there was constant blood-letting between one group or another."

"So why did you remain? Surely your assignments permit some coming and going."

"For the most part, but this one was out of the ordinary. My initial tour was about to end—some nine or ten months ago—when I engineered a dialogue between some of the tribal leaders. It started when one of the more recalcitrant factions decided to talk to Bill and me, probably hoping to get their propaganda publicized. But it was a breakthrough and the State Department asked us to remain to see if we would help keep the peace negotiations going. They also cautioned us about revealing our role to anyone, even our families. We could do nothing that might break the faith.

"I knew staying wasn't fair to B.J., but I had to consider other children, those whose lives were being affected daily by what was happening there. Every night I went to sleep hoping that the next day I could come home and explain it all to him."

"I take it that negotiations eventually broke down?"

"Enough for the two of us to finally try to get out of there and for Bill to get a bullet on the way. I believe they've resumed since then—as fragile as ever, but at least we're no part of it. As soon as I got to England, I arranged for a sabbatical so I could spend some time in Texas getting reacquainted with my son. It took me a few weeks longer to get here than I'd expected, what with debriefings and closing out my office." Clark picked up his coffee cup, changed his mind and set it back on the table. "So there you have it. End of story." Giving a shrug, he leaned back against the couch, stretching his legs at an angle in front of him so the tips of his boots would miss the coffee table.

Jan suspected there was a great deal more to it, but she did believe him and she had to respect his choice. It hadn't been easy for B.J., but it didn't seem to have been easy for Clark, either. "Then when you finally got back, you found out that everything here had changed."

"Yeah, so instead of the sabbatical, I resigned from the network."

"Resigned?"

"It seemed the thing to do. My life's in Valentine from now on, Jan. That's why I bought the land—to settle on. Even though the Phillips' house leaves something to be desired." He chuckled. "Have you ever seen the place?"

She shook her head.

"To say it's a wreck is a compliment. That's why I haven't moved. Zeke Phillips never spent a dime on repairs as far as I can tell. I don't think that house has seen paint since the original coat was applied, and the plumbing's so old, it rumbles like a subway passing through. I'm still trying to decide whether to renovate or tear everything down and start all over. But it's home sweet home now. Or will be as soon as we can get something habitable."

We, he'd said, the implication clear that his son would live with him. "Do you plan to operate a working ranch?"

"I don't know. I guess I haven't thought that far ahead."

She'd have felt better if he'd told her that, yes, he wanted to run Santa Gertrudis or Herefords, or raise quarter horses. Obviously there were no well-thought-out plans, no long-term goals. Despite his claim of "the die being cast," it sounded more like a spur-of-the-moment purchase, a whim. Something that with a little effort could be undone.

His answer gave no confirmation of permanency. As she'd thought previously, Clark would eventually need a new challenge of some sort and certainly at some point, he'd need an income. "I imagine it'll take a lot to get everything going again," she said.

He nodded. "A lot of time and a lot of money. I've got the time—or is it the money you're wondering about? Asking yourself how I can afford to stay here, unemployed, so to speak?"

"Your financial situation isn't my—" The mocking look on Clark's face caused her to pause. "I suppose it did cross my mind," she finally admitted.

"I can afford it."

Jan realized she'd been incredibly rude probing into his private business. "I didn't mean to be so nosy."

"But you were, so I'm going to tell you and set your mind to rest."

"My mind is okay. You don't have to 'rest' it."

"Oh, but I do. I'm going to make sure you don't have any room for doubt—about this or anything else. In the first place, my out-of-pocket expenses have been minimal for quite a while. It's hard to go on a spending spree in a Saudi desert or in the foothills of some god-forsaken country where bullets fly hourly. As a result, other than what I've sent Toni and B.J., the bulk of my salary has been invested."

Jan's skepticism mounted. Money—big money, the amount it would take to purchase Clark's ranch and make it function—didn't come from invested salary. That kind of booty required a hefty inheritance or a winning lottery ticket or a financial venture of interest to law enforcement officials. She didn't know much about Clark's background, but she doubted he was heir to a fortune. No one in this rumor mill of a town had mentioned family money, or lottery winnings, either. That only left crime.

"I've got a job, Jan." Clark's voice interrupted her capricious speculations.

"A job? Here?"

"It's the kind of job that can be done anywhere, as long as I've got a computer and access to a post office. Even before I learned about Toni's death and decided I was needed in Valentine, a publisher had contacted me about writing a book. One positive thing to come out of my experiences in Africa is that they make a good first-person story. He offered me a contract and I accepted. In fact, I've even had some feelers about a possible movie for television."

Jan took a deep breath as Clark's explanation sank in. He might not be here forever, but it generally took a year or two to write a book; Clark wouldn't be departing anytime soon. For some reason the news was both comforting and frightening.

"So now you have a chapter of my life story—or at least the salient parts. Now let's talk about you."

She shook her head. "I'm afraid I have no tale to match yours. I wouldn't even attempt to compete." Jan put down her glass and stood. The only thing Clark didn't know about her involved Glen, and if she could prevent it, that subject would not come up. "Anyway, it's late. I think we've talked enough tonight." She was halfway across the room when Clark stopped her and wheeled her around.

"I totally agree. We've talked enough." His voice was soft and husky and his hands had worked their way behind her to pull her close. "Am I tempting fate if I kiss you?" he asked.

"Not as far as I'm concerned," she whispered as she accepted his lips eagerly, her arms encircling his neck. He might have caught her by surprise just now, but she'd been building up to this moment all day. For the first time they shared a kiss without rancor and without the infringement of outside forces. She eagerly pressed against him, her body on fire, the pent-up passion confined so long, bursting forth.

Clark ended the kiss and stroked her cheek. "Whatever you might think, that was the extent of the lovemaking I'd hoped for this evening. I didn't get B.J. out of the house to seduce you—much as I want to." He turned her toward the door. "Good night, Jan."

Momentarily, Jan just stood there, not knowing what to do. Part of her wanted to run like demons were chasing her, another part wanted to be pulled back into Clark's arms. Of all times for him to be so noble. Reluctantly she left the den, without looking back.

Upstairs she lay in bed, thinking about Clark and how all her defenses seemed to have melted away. She spent restless hours, trying to deal with her conflicting feelings. For Garrett's sake, she wanted to maintain her distance from Clark, but she no longer could. Clark may have made mistakes, but who hadn't? The past few days she'd seen sides of him she could only describe as admirable. He'd been so impressively attentive to B.J., firm when necessary but lenient, too. And the child was responding positively. Without a doubt Clark was winning B.J. over, slowly mending the rift caused by the time they'd spent apart.

Yet Jan cautioned herself to be wary, to remember that Clark's interest—in B.J. *and* in her—might be only fleeting. For B.J.'s sake, she hoped not. For her own.... She'd vowed not to become involved with a man—not for a long while anyway. But Jan's heart was no longer cooperating with her resolve.

Instead it kept drifting back to that latest kiss—ending so much differently than before—and on to all the wondrous things that happened when one fell in love. Could that be happening to her? Jan knew it was a distinct possibility. Her growing affection for Clark couldn't be denied.

Clark was just finishing breakfast when she came down for hers. Jan had dallied in her room, hoping he would be outside by this time. Strangely, now that she'd reluctantly acknowledged her emotions to herself, she felt shy toward him. She tersely responded to his "good morning" and walked over to pour a cup of coffee. The syrupy brew looked like it had been simmering for three days.

She purposely kept her back turned as Clark donned his coat and hat, but his reflection in the adjacent window told her he was smiling as he approached the sink to deposit his dishes. She was still monitoring his movements in the glass when he came up behind her and placed his hands on her shoulders. Without speaking, he turned her toward him and kissed her. This time his kiss was light, playful, but its effect no less disturbing to her than the one the night before.

She was still in a trance minutes after he'd turned her loose and disappeared wordlessly out the back door.

"Is it time for school?" B.J.'s coming in the back door jolted her from her reverie.

She was grateful for the interruption. The two of them went off to the classroom and the activities of teaching occupied Jan's mind for the next several hours.

Midway into morning, the glare of a bright sun flashed through the blinds, making a pattern across the room where Jan and B.J. worked. She put down the piece of chalk she was using and went to look outside. The condensation on the glass had disappeared, revealing unblemished blue skies, and a dripping icicle told her that the temperature must be climbing.

By noon the rotund snow family had begun to melt into nothingness, as if its members had been on crash diets. More tufts of withered grass were visible on the front lawn as the white covering evaporated. Surely the roads had cleared sufficiently for her to make it home safely, as long as she kept a cautious eye for patches of ice. Jan didn't know whether to be sorry or relieved that it was time to go, but she was aware that she needed a separation from Clark to sort through her emotions.

Jan quickly packed her few belongings in a paper sack and said goodbye to B.J. and Rue Nell. She was gone shortly after midday.

The roads were still hazardous, but she made the drive to town without incident, going directly to the post office. She'd alerted Sally that she was coming in and knew her aunt would worry until assured that she'd arrived in one piece. Pulling her Mitsubishi into a parking place right beside a big white Chrysler, Jan switched off the key and glanced up at the man emerging from the post office.

Garrett. A pang of guilt hit her. She'd given precious little thought to his problems in the last few days.

Jan felt even more ashamed when she met him on the sidewalk. He removed his hat before giving her a big smothering hug. "Are you okay, honey?" Holding her at arm's length, he seemed to be inspecting her for telltale signs of distress. "Do you forgive me for deserting you this week? I should have heeded the weather reports, but those danged forecasters are wrong more often than not. Wouldn't you know that this time they'd hit it right on the button?"

She stood on tiptoe to kiss his cheek. "As you well know, there's nothing to forgive. Although I have to admit, I'd have preferred having you around." *At first, anyway*.

"You didn't have any trouble with Brennan?"

"Of course not." She could tell from Garrett's grimace that a strong denial was necessary.

"Well, if he bothers you, let me know. I've heard tales about him and the ladies. And Lord knows, Toni was blinded by him for a long time."

Jan felt let down. Clearly the hours in Austin had not softened the rancher toward his former son-in-law. He crooked a finger under her chin so he could meet her eyes. "You're sure everything's okay?"

"Positive," she lied.

"Well, if he starts trifling with you, Jan, I'll put a stop to it." Garrett settled his Stetson back on his head and bade her goodbye.

Jan had undergone a thorough interrogation by the time she got home. First Garrett, and then Sally who had been unable to squelch her interest about Jan's time at the ranch. Her enthusiastic questions and the intense look in her eyes made Jan uncomfortable. Was she crazy or did her aunt seem to be promoting a relationship between her and Clark?

Obviously, the pull of the upcoming holiday had come into play. With Sally, romance would triumph over practicality any day of the year, but it was worse in February. That's when all logic became suspended. Jan wondered whether she'd also succumbed to the season and lost all common sense.

Garrett called soon after Jan arrived home, telling her not to drive to the ranch the next day. "The roads will glaze back over tonight. No need to take chances with your safety."

Having the next day alone was good for her. Jan put aside her fretting and concentrated instead on the things she enjoyed—an extended bubble bath, reading, cooking, a trip to the backyard. Happily, she discovered that the plants had survived the winter blast without any significant frost damage.

It was late afternoon and celery soup was bubbling on the kitchen stove when she heard Sally's Jeep pull under the carport.

"Hi, hon. How was your day?"

"Fine. You're earlier than I expected."

"The work's finally under control. Like I told you this morning, we didn't need any more help."

Sally removed her coat, revealing one of the numerous red outfits she wore in keeping with the holiday spirit. Today she was bedecked in a red and white checkered pantsuit.

"By the way, I talked to Garrett earlier. From what I could tell he gave you the day off mainly to keep you out of the fray—figured he and Clark would be going tooth and nail. I suspect that despite Garrett's objections, Clark's going to be a permanent fixture around here. So how do you feel about that?" Sally looked intently at Jan.

"It's of little concern to me," Jan said dismissively, then quite deliberately changed the subject. "If you're heading back to work, I can tag along."

Although she knew her aunt had no intention of working any later today, Jan couldn't resist goading her. It was canasta party night—the only event besides church that could entice Sally away from work right now. Trivial Pursuit and Scrabble might be the games of choice in metropolitan Dallas or Houston, but in many ways Valentine fixated on an earlier, simpler time. The women of Sally's generation played canasta with the same fervor as they had since its heyday in the fifties. Naturally gossip was an integral part of all the games.

Sally crooked an eyebrow, wise to Jan's ribbing, and shook her head as she went off to her bedroom to change. To another bright red outfit, of course.

Once her aunt was out of sight, Jan's thoughts flitted back to Sally's question about Clark. Would he really stay longer than just the time to write his book? Sally had an impressive knack for reading people and predicting their behavior. And if she were right, what did that mean for Jan? Doubts or no, Jan knew her attraction to the man wasn't going away.

How did Clark feel, or did he care about her at all? Flirting came naturally to him, and a few stolen kisses signified nothing. Even if they did, Jan realized getting involved with Clark Brennan might be the worst thing that could happen. Yet she knew she was headed precisely in that direction. So what was she to do?

Keeping out of his way wasn't a solution. The last few days were evidence of that. Of course, if Clark won custody, she might not be teaching B.J. any longer. He might have other plans. But there was still church, the grocery, social events...all those other places where they'd come together. In a small town she could hardly pretend Clark didn't exist.

So, if he did stick around, what then? Could she remain in Valentine with unresolved sentiments about him constantly gnawing at her? Jan suspected she knew the answer.

"Oh, well," she said aloud. "I never planned to stay here forever." It was time to update her résumé and start looking at job advertisements. The state education agency could probably give her some ideas about which school districts were hiring. She would also check out some private academies.

Teachers were in demand. With luck, she'd land a job elsewhere. She might not find the new position as satisfying as being "Miss Jan" on television or tutoring B.J., but she'd have no trouble earning a living. Yet try as she might to put on a happy face, tonight she was having a difficult time. She felt tense, melancholy.

Sally was off to her card party and Jan had just settled down to dinner and *Wheel of Fortune* when she heard a car pull up. Somehow, she knew it was Clark. She met him at the door.

He gave her that irrepressible grin. "I realize I'm intruding at suppertime again, but things weren't too pleasant at the ranch and I needed to escape."

"What makes you think it'll be any more pleasant here?" She felt annoyed again, mostly at herself for being so elated to see him. It was only for protection's sake that she'd tossed a barb his way.

"I decided to take my chances. The only choices were either your place or Annette's Diner. At least here I'm not risking being drawn into an interminable domino game. Or having to fend off nosy questions about my plans. Or both." He followed her into the kitchen and draped his coat over a chair.

Jan had started to blurt out a smart-aleck remark about how flattering she found his reason for selecting her, then something in Clark's face stopped her. Despite his cool mien, she could see that, underneath, he was agitated. Most of the time he did a masterful job of taking events in stride. Thus it concerned her to see him this way. "Have you eaten?" she asked solicitously, leading the way into the kitchen.

"No, but I'm not really hungry. Thanks, anyway. You go ahead."

She added a ladle of warm soup to her bowl and started back to the porch. Clark trailed along behind and once there, eased down in the wicker rocking chair, staring at the television as she ate.

"This is a nice room," he commented, although he hardly seemed aware of where they were. It appeared more like an effort at making conversation than a serious observation.

Jan went along with him though. "Yes, my aunt had it enclosed a couple of years ago. We spend a lot of time here."

"Where is she tonight? Out playing matchmaker?"

"Not tonight—cards—but she does have a tendency to do the other, too." From Clark's comment, Jan wondered how actively Sally had been engaging in that particular endeavor today. She'd had that weird look on her face earlier and she'd kept probing about Jan and Clark. Not your typical Sally. It *would* be typical Sally, however, to decide to attempt a match-up between them, even over Garrett's objections.

Clark picked up the newspaper and scanned the headlines. It was the local weekly and Jan couldn't control her interest as she studied his face. A seasoned reporter like Clark would be terribly amused at what Valentine considered news. There was the story about Mrs. Burleson's granddaughter visiting from St. Louis and a write-up about last week's canasta party. The paper might appear simplistic to someone as sophisticated as Clark, but it was what the people in Valentine wanted. For hard news, they turned to the dailies from the cities.

Jan watched him continue his perusal of the pages as she took the last few spoonfuls of soup and nibbled on her sandwich. He wasn't smiling or laughing as she'd expected. In fact, he wasn't responding at all. Finally, she pushed the tray aside. It was obvious that he didn't even know what he was reading. "Want to tell me what's wrong?" She switched off the television.

"Huh?"

"Tell me what happened between you and Garrett."

He looked at her warily. "I realize our conflict is not your problem."

"No, but you want to talk about it anyway, right?"

"Yeah, I need to talk to someone." He scowled. "You wouldn't believe what that old fool's gone and done."

Jan bridled at the insult. She might be feeling sympathetic toward Clark at the moment, but she also had to remain loyal to her friend. "Garrett Montgomery is a fine man and I can't allow you to insult him that way. If that's what you came to do, I won't put up with it." She rose to her feet as if to tell him it was time to go, overresponding as usual with Clark.

Clark stood up, too. "There you go again. I should have known you wouldn't be any more rational than he's being. But after what's happened between you and me...." His voice trailed off.

"Nothing's happened." *Oh, boy, am I telling a big one.*

"You're wrong. I know you're trying to deny the possibility," he said, seeing right through her. "But a lot's going on between us and you know it. We'll leave that for another time though. A time when you can think for yourself instead of being blinded by loyalty to Garrett. My *father-in-law...your fine man*...filed a court motion declaring me an unfit father."

"No. I don't believe it." Stunned, she sat back down. Surely, she'd have been told if he had, yet neither Garrett nor Sally had said one word.

"It's true. That's what his trip to Austin was all about—beating the bushes for an attorney to handle his case. He's not content to share B.J. He wants the boy all to himself, most likely to spoil, just like he did Toni. Well, I won't have it. If Garrett wants a fight, then he's going to find me one hell of an opponent."

"A lot of good that'll do your son. Haven't you seen how tormented he is when the two of you are squabbling?"

"I'm aware of his suffering, but I didn't start this. I've tried my damnedest to get along, to go along."

Jan felt obligated to play devil's advocate. "Oh, right. Is buying the very ranch that Garrett's coveted for years what you call getting along?"

"I did it for my son—no other reason. And there was no way on God's green earth Zeke was ever going to sell to Garrett. Everyone's told me so—even you. Garrett ought to be relieved *I* was the buyer and not some commercial pig farm. Zeke could have really dealt Garrett misery if he'd tried."

Jan racked her brain for a snappy comeback. She wanted to argue with Clark. It was less risky to be at odds with him than to acknowledge the feelings she was harboring. She knew that his purchase of the property adjoining the Montgomery ranch had been a good faith effort. And while he had made mistakes as a father, "unfit" was a label Clark didn't deserve. "So what are you going to do now?"

"What choice do I have? I can either defend myself or risk losing B.J. That's not going to happen. I'm not going to be separated from him again." He sat down on the sofa beside her, taking her hand in his. "I know how much you care about Garrett Montgomery, so I know what I'm asking of you. Still, I have to ask. Will you help me, Jan? Will you help me keep my boy?"

CHAPTER ELEVEN

How could she say yes? Garrett's actions might be rash, but to betray him by helping Clark was unconscionable.

"You don't realize what you're asking," she responded, pulling her hands from his.

"Only that you help me do what's best for my son."

"Are you sure keeping him from Garrett is best?"

"If I wanted to 'keep him from Garrett' I wouldn't have bought the ranch next door. I just refuse to forfeit my role as B.J.'s father."

What he said made sense, but she dared not trust her own judgment. Especially since it seemed to flip-flop one hundred and eighty degrees depending on whether she was with Clark or with Garrett. Also, she couldn't stop making comparisons between Clark and her former husband.

Men like Glen and Clark could convince women the world was flat if they put their minds to it. Was she letting Clark's charm get in the way of logic? As she well knew, charm was short-lived, mere window-dressing. It was no indication of dependability. Right now B.J. was a novelty for his father, a novelty that could wear thin. But, determined as she might be to make such a case, Jan's argument held little merit. Clark had conducted himself admirably with his son. There was no longer a reason to question his sincerity or commitment.

Jan was torn. Aligning herself with Clark carried a big penalty. By doing so, she'd alienate her dearest friend in Valentine, to say nothing of the potential impact on aunt. Sally's romantic hints aside, she had an otional tie with Garrett that could suffer irreparable damage if Jan did something to sabotage it.

Clark reached out and, for the second time, took her hands in his. "I'm not asking for myself, but for B.J. As his teacher, your first duty is to your pupil."

"You don't need to remind me of my duty," she said angrily. Again Jan pulled her hands away, feeling compromised by his touch and the intimacy that went with it. She had to remain objective, react coolly to his plea. "And what if I sincerely believe that Garrett should prevail in this lawsuit?"

"If you honestly suggested that I should be declared an unfit father, I'd probably throw in the towel right now. But you're not suggesting that, are you, Jan?" He eased closer, draping an arm across the back of the couch. "B.J. and I have bonded. You said so yourself."

"I don't deny I've seen some progress."

"And is there some progress between you and me, too?"

The remark raised her suspicions again. Why make a point of their relationship now? She remembered Clark's boasting that he'd "checkmated" Garrett when he bought the Phillips land. Could his romancing her have been plotted like a real-life chess game, with her in the role of a pawn? Had his actions at the ranch been a calculated effort to win her over? After living through a similar situation with Glen, she had no intention of being used and manipulated by another smooth talker, especially one she'd known barely two weeks.

"I will not be drawn into your war with Garrett," she said with finality.

"And you think by turning me down you can avoid it? Think again. You'll be forced to choose sides. If not mine, then Garrett's. He'll be urging you to support him, to say all sorts of rotten things about me."

She leaned forward to meet his gaze head-on. "That won't happen. Garrett Montgomery is a gentleman. He'd never pressure me to say or do anything I didn't feel comfortable with."

Clark snorted with derision. "Don't make me laugh. Garrett's a Texas rancher, and let's face it, a very savvy businessman. You may see him as an old softie, but he's tough as nails when he has to be. He's used to winning and the stakes are high in this game, very high. After all, this is his grandchild—and there won't be another. He'll do whatever it takes to get your backing, including a subpoena, if necessary. So, the question remains, my naive little Jan, who do you plan to support—Garrett or B.J.?"

Caught short, she hesitated for a moment, then composed herself enough to raise a derisive eyebrow. "And what about Clark Brennan? You left him out of the equation." She got up and walked over to the window.

"My interests are the same as my son's," Clark said, his voice testy.

"You're certain of that?" Again the raised eyebrow.

"Being with me has been good for the boy...you can't deny it. You know how much he's responded, and in just a matter of days. He *needs* me."

"He's *needed* you for a long time and you weren't there for him. What's going to happen when you go running off like before?"

"Who says I'll be running off?"

"Your past says it."

"What does it take to convince you I've changed—a blood oath?" He jumped up, exasperation marking his features. "Get this straight. I'm not going to pull out of my son's life. I'm here for the duration." The lines in his face softened, along with his voice. "Now for the last time, will you help me?"

Jan thought she'd left turmoil behind in Los Angeles. But it had followed. The notion of Valentine as a peaceful haven evaporated like dew on a spring morning. She didn't know what to do. A part of her was influenced by loyalty to Garrett. Another part—a more compelling part—leaned toward Clark.

"Will you?" His soft blue eyes were almost pleading.

She turned toward the window and stared out into the darkness, needing the moment's respite to escape the hypnotizing force of his gaze. "At this point I can't answer," she finally said, looking back at him. "I need to think about it."

An unexpected smile suddenly appeared on his face. She'd anticipated more argument—instead Clark seemed pleased and satisfied, as if she'd made a commitment to him.

"I'm not promising anything," she reminded him. "I only agreed to think it over."

"That's enough." He came over and grasped her shoulders, as though he was going to embrace her, but he dropped his hands without doing so. "I have faith that you'll do the right thing." He walked toward the kitchen to retrieve his jacket. "I don't want to rush you, but I need an answer tomorrow, before this escalates any further. B.J. and I will be at our place working. Why don't you come by for lunch?"

One day to reach a decision? When she'd asked for time, Jan had been thinking about a week or two—or more. How could she weigh all her options in less than twenty-four hours? It would take a Solomon to arrive at a solution in that amount of time. "I don't know...."

"Come if you can," Clark said, not pushing the matter. Instead he simply picked up his jacket and left.

Leaning against the closed door, she listened to the start of the car engine and the crunch of the tires on the gravel drive. And still she didn't move. Long after the sounds of the motor faded into the distance, Jan remained there, her mind too muddled to send her body a simple command like *sit down*.

Clark was right when he said neutrality wasn't an option. She would have to indicate a preference in favor of one of the two men.

If choosing was all she had to wrestle with, it'd be difficult enough. But it was much more complicated than that. Her responsibility to B.J. was the foremost consideration, of course. But those other allegiances couldn't be treated lightly. How could she do what was right for B.J. and still be fair to both his father and grandfather? It didn't seem possible.

Jan worked at the post office on Saturday. All of Sally's temporary helpers were present this last weekend before the Valentine holiday, and the atmosphere was party-like, the employees high-spirited. Peggy had baked heart-shaped sugar cookies and Yvonne brought spiced tea in a Crockpot. Everyone wore red, of course, including Jan who sported a gift from Sally—a white sweat shirt decorated with dozens of tiny red hearts.

The townspeople, too, were in the spirit, stopping by in their red shirts and blouses, the women with dangling heart earrings and valentine pins. Even the mayor dropped in, a necktie decorated with battery-lit hearts draped proudly over his huge belly.

Despite the socializing, the main activity remained moving the mail. Every card was scheduled to be stamped and readied for shipping out on Tuesday, Sally Mac's "D" day, or "V" day, as she called it. "Here's one from Paris, France." The postmistress handed Jan an envelope covered in tiny red hearts. "Can you imagine?"

"You're world famous," Jan answered. Her statement was not a total exaggeration. The cards did come from all over. She supposed there could even be one here from Glen, intended for some other woman.

Now what made me think of him? For months she'd wondered about Glen, about where he'd gone and what he was doing, every question bringing a wave of pain. Recently she hadn't thought of him much at all and even when she did, remembering no longer caused so much as a twinge. She tried to ignore the significance, but it was there all the same. If she reminisced about Glen less frequently, if the hurt had disappeared, it was because her thoughts were on someone else. Right now the implications of that were more disturbing than anything that had happened in her past.

"Just imagine what's in those cards," Sally twittered. "Marriage proposals...declarations of undying love...probably some X-rated messages, too." Her voice interrupted Jan's thoughts. "Aside from those naughty ones, if I had my way, I'd snoop and read every last one of them."

Jan looked askance at her. "Don't give me that. You know full well you wouldn't even if the cards came in unsealed."

"No, you're right," Sally agreed. Then she grinned. "But that doesn't mean I wouldn't like to...."

As the clock neared twelve, Jan prepared to leave. "Are you coming home?" she asked Sally.

"No, dear. Margaret and I are going to a movie in Temple. Want to tag along?"

"Not today." Jan gave her aunt a hug, relieved that Sally had plans. Now there was no need to explain her destination this afternoon. Jan was going to take Clark up on his invitation for lunch. She told herself she needed to check out where B.J. would be living. That was as good a rationalization as any.

Had she not seen it with her own eyes, Jan would have refused to believe snow and ice had covered the landscape only days before. All traces had melted away and spring was making a second effort to appear. Jan looked over the rolling meadows as she drove. According to Sally, soon they would be blanketed with bluebonnets and the roadsides dotted with scarlet Indian paintbrushes, yellow stick leaf and dozens of other wildflowers. It would be Jan's first spring in Texas, a time she'd looked forward to since learning about the state's commitment to wildflowers—a legacy fostered by Lady Bird Johnson during her husband's term as President, and continued on after their retirement in Texas.

Jan hadn't attempted to secure directions for reaching Clark's new home since there was no way to do so without revealing her intentions and fueling more gossip. She knew that the land adjoined Garrett's and figured that was knowledge enough to enable her to find it. However, after driving several miles past the turnoff to Garrett's home, Jan began to fear she was lost. A feeling of relief eased over her when she topped a hill and saw in the distance a ranch house, with a barn and outbuildings off to the side. This had to be the Phillips' place.

From her vantage point, Jan spied an unfamiliar red pickup parked in the neighboring pasture. As she approached a fence separating Clark's acreage from

Garrett's, she saw Clark and B.J. outside the vehicle. They appeared to be loading a section of wire fence.

Clark spotted her, then stopped to whisper something to the child. Immediately both of them waved and she pulled to the side of the road.

As she made her way through a dirt gully to join them, Jan was glad that she'd chosen to wear a pair of old boots. Clark came over to assist her, pulling her up the bank and spreading apart the barbed wire of the roadside fence for her to crawl between. He didn't comment on the fact she was here, but his expression was one of unexpected pleasure, as though he hadn't been sure she would come.

"What are you two doing?" she asked, bending down to accept B.J.'s hug.

"I thought removing the fence might help," Clark told her. "B.J. agrees." He turned toward the little boy who nodded.

"Grandpa's been mad because Mr. Phillips wouldn't let him get to the river. We fixed it so the cows can walk right over there for a drink." He pointed toward a copse of mesquite trees a few hundred yards away. "Now maybe Grandpa won't be mad at Daddy anymore. Speckles can get through, too." He picked up a set of wire clippers and went back over to the fence, his small hands unsuccessfully trying to snip another section of the barrier.

Clark gave Jan a quick wink. "He may not be making much progress, but he deserves an A for effort."

"The fence *does* belong to you, doesn't it?"

"Don't worry. I checked it out and every post is on my property. I don't want any more good intentions boomeranging on me."

"Then I think it's a great idea."

"At least it's worth a try," Clark agreed. "Like you said, if Garrett and I can't settle this between us, B.J.'s going to be the one to suffer. I don't want him to think he can't love us both. That's what happened to me. Whenever I spent time with my mother I was betraying my father. When I was with Dad, Mom was upset with me. Whatever it takes to save B.J. from that kind of conflict, I'll do." He eyed her solemnly. "That's a promise, Jan."

She believed him. The gesture of taking down the fence was just another step toward convincing her that Clark really meant to get along with Garrett. She wasn't sure that Garrett would accept the olive branch just yet, but maybe eventually. She felt more optimistic—everything could work out after all. It might even work out before she had to take sides.

"We'll drive up to the house for lunch. Rue Nell packed some sandwich stuff for us." He cast a glance B.J.'s way. "My junior assistant's been at it long enough. I can't have him getting blisters."

The ride took only a few minutes and Clark parked in the dirt drive. "Like I told you, it's a mess. Zeke sure wasn't angling for a feature in *Better Homes and Gardens*."

"It is an eyesore," Jan agreed, approaching the rickety front steps. Clark was right, the gray weather-worn exterior looked as if it hadn't seen a paintbrush in thirty years, and several boards on the front porch were rotted through.

"Be careful," Clark said, taking her elbow. "Fortunately, the interior's in better shape." He pushed open the front door.

The two-story house was large, with an entry hall roomy enough to stash a grand piano in the corner and not crowd the stairway curving to the second floor. Flanking the entry was a living room on one side and what appeared to be a den on the other. Directly in front of them was a formal dining area, a massive oak table still in place.

"That was Zeke's. He didn't want to go to the trouble of moving it," Clark said, stirring a cloud of dust with a swipe of his hand across its surface. "Since I own no furniture, that was fine with me. It's one less thing I have to worry about. Let's go to the kitchen." He directed her down a hallway as B.J. scampered in front of them. The kitchen, like the other rooms, was in dire need of renovation. The countertops, sink and cabinets were stained and scratched and the flooring was a faded linoleum.

"I've got someone coming over next week to put in a new hot water heater and check out all the plumbing. First we'll get this kitchen updated and some modern bathrooms installed. I'm not sure what should come next."

"Definitely the porch," Jan suggested, bringing a grin to Clark's face.

"The porch." He grasped B.J. on the shoulder. "The way B.J. and I see it, it'll take three or four years before we have the place like we want it. I envision it painted white, maybe with black shutters, a lawn—"

"And a tree house," B.J. interrupted.

"A tree house," Clark echoed.

He opened a food basket on the countertop. Without being asked, Jan took over serving the sandwiches.

While she arranged the food on paper plates, B.J. popped open cans of Coke from a cooler and Clark dragged in boxes to serve as makeshift table and chairs. The three ate companionably, B.J. more talkative than Jan had witnessed before. He was becoming an absolute chatterbox and was visibly happy to be with his father, even if chores were involved.

After lunch, the three toured the house. As they climbed to the second floor, Clark assured her the stairs were safe regardless of the creaks she heard with every footfall on the risers. Once they reached the landing, B.J. immediately deserted them, running through one of the bedrooms and opening French doors to play on a terrace. He emptied several toy cars from his pocket and started rolling them across the wood.

"That terrace is becoming his favorite place," Clark said, "and before you begin to worry, don't. It's secure out there, too. Actually, everything is structurally sound except the front porch."

Despite her earlier conclusion that Clark had made no plans, it was clear that he'd given a great deal of attention to the living arrangements. He was almost gushing about what was to take place.

She'd become caught up in his fervor, unable to keep from offering a couple of suggestions: skylights to brighten those rooms with too few windows, replacement of the outdated light fixtures with ceiling fans. It would be a lovely home once Clark was finished.

"I promised to get B.J. back. He and Garrett are going into town for haircuts. Will you wait for me?"

Jan wasn't certain that was a good idea, but she agreed anyway. She was impatient to know the latest happenings between Clark and Garrett and there hadn't been an opportunity for discussions without B.J. overhearing. From what she could tell, though, there must have been some improvement between the two men—or at least, a temporary state of détente.

She hoped so, anyway. The prospect of being pulled in as some kind of character assassin by Garrett was distasteful to her as well as a waste of time for Garrett. She no longer felt antagonistic toward Clark. Quite the opposite—she was beginning to be downright admiring. B.J. was a different child from the one he'd been before Clark came. The youngster talked and laughed more and the tantrums had completely abated. Those were the plain facts.

Yet challenging Garrett seemed just as unsettling. The alliance with Clark could backfire. What if he were offered an exciting assignment in some exotic place? Never mind good intentions, would a book contract, a broken-down ranch and his son keep him in Texas? Jan didn't know the answer.

It took less than a half hour for Clark to return. "Do you want to walk down by the river?"

Jan nodded and he took her hand as they ambled through the meadow.

The "river" was a slight exaggeration. It was more like a small stream of water meandering through a rock-ladened bed, a few small pools slowing its course. Clark gestured to a couple of boulders on the bank and they sat down.

"Has there been a reconciliation between you and Garrett?" she asked.

"Not really. He's stopped yelling and hasn't kicked me out of the house, so I guess that's something. Frankly, after hearing about the motion he'd filed, I started packing to move out, except I had no place where I could take B.J. So I've had to swallow my pride and hang on awhile." Clark scooped up a fistful of pebbles. "He's going back to talk to those lawyers on Monday...who knows what will happen then."

"Maybe the best thing for now is just to wait and see."

"Perhaps you're right, but it's not easy." He sent one of the stones plopping into a pool of water, then repeated the action. Minutes passed without conversation. Finally Clark said, "Jan, tell me about the trouble in Los Angeles, about the trial and your husband leaving L.A."

"How did you learn about that?" The change of subject had blindsided her. Although she'd shared some tidbits of information with Clark, she'd deliberately omitted the parts about Glen dumping her and dropping from sight.

Clark shrugged.

"You've been checking on me, haven't you?"

When he shrugged again, she continued. "Sneaking around like some cheesy tabloid reporter." She stood up and glared down at him, hands on hips. "Of all the contemptible things to do! I hope learning all the lurid details has made you happy."

"Not particularly." Clark plopped another pebble into the water before standing, also. "How could it make me happy knowing what a difficult time you went through, how hurt you were?"

"Enough of the good guy routine. I'm not buying it anymore. What you did was devious and underhanded. And you damn well know it!" She took a deep breath. *How could he have invaded her privacy like this*? "Not that it's any of your business, but if you wanted...if you had to.... Why didn't you just ask me?"

"I did ask. Every time I tried to ferret out a detail or two, you clammed up. And whether you like the idea or not, I do consider you my business."

"So how did you find out?"

"A newspaper friend in Los Angeles provided me with the details that you wouldn't. I wanted to know why you were hurting, Jan. I *needed* to know."

"And for what reason? Plain old meddling or fodder for a chapter in your second book? The book on disasters, I suppose. Or maybe on scandals. Am I going to be used to increase sales?"

Clark's eyes met hers. "You know I'd never do that."

"You're wrong." Jan turned her head away. She felt tears welling in her eyes and she didn't want Clark to see how he'd violated her with his snooping. "I know nothing of the sort." She forced her voice to be steady. "Actually I don't know you well enough to say for sure *what* you're capable of."

"I thought we were fixing that. A bit more time, a bit more sharing...."

"No, thank you. I think you've discovered too much about me already. All I need is for you to stay away from me and quit poking into my life. Now I'm leaving before I say something I shouldn't." She stood up and started toward her car, Clark right on her heels.

"I'll take the risk of your tongue-lashing," he told her, "if I can get you to face facts."

"I have faced them. I've agonized over the past until I'm sick of it. Now it's over and done with. So what can be gained by bringing up matters that I've tried to put behind me?"

"You've put nothing behind you. You're toting the past on your shoulders like a precious fur stole that you don't dare take off. You've got to cast it aside and get on with your life."

"My life was getting along just fine, until you came into it. Why don't you just go away and leave us all alone?"

For a second, Clark's face clouded as the remark hit home, but he quickly recovered. He leaned in closer, his nose almost touching hers. "You don't really want me to leave you alone, do you, Jan? There's something between us—we both recognized it the minute I peered over that post office counter and saw you on the floor surrounded by valentines."

"You have quite an imagination."

"Don't you believe in love, Jan?"

"We're not talking about love."

"Aren't we?"

Jan couldn't stop the tingle that sped down her spine at the word *love* and when he pulled her into his arms, her inclination was to lift her lips to his. But such a move on her part would lead to more complications than she could handle. "Don't," she pleaded.

"I'm only going to kiss you." His voice was gentle.

"That's what I'm afraid of—" Jan stopped, realizing that she'd verified Clark's statement about something between them. "I really do need to get home." She pointed at the sky. "It'll be dark soon and...."

As her words trailed off, he took her hand and silently walked her back to her car, taking her keys and unlocking the door. There he brushed his lips across her cheek, then pulled her tight against his chest. Jan could hear the rapid beat of his heart; hers no doubt sounded the same way. She pushed away from him and entered the car, purposefully focusing her eyes straight ahead and avoiding any glances through the rearview mirror as she drove toward home.

Neither Clark, Garrett nor B.J. was in church the next morning. Their absence worried Jan—it wasn't like Garrett and B.J. to miss a Sunday. Sally didn't seem concerned though, so Jan just let the matter drop. Making an issue of it would have Sally wondering what had her so worked up.

The church service dragged on endlessly and all the rest of Sunday passed excruciatingly slow, like a watched clock. Jan found the forced leisure oppressive and was annoyed at herself for jumping whenever the telephone rang. Each time she anticipated it to be Clark. It never was.

She was glad when Monday finally arrived and she could get back to the ranch. She tried to convince herself that devotion to her duties was kindling her interest, but in this instance Jan knew her tutoring job was incidental. Over all her best instincts and efforts, she'd flipped over Clark, at the same time recognizing that she could be making one of the biggest mistakes of her life.

Clark's rental car wasn't there when she arrived on Monday, nor that red pickup. But she didn't really expect them to be. Clark was likely at his own place, already meeting with the workmen to begin remodeling the house. She didn't see Garrett, either. According to B.J., he was out tending the cattle.

Jan wasn't sure what had occurred on Sunday, but whatever it was, her pupil seemed to be taking it in his stride. He was attentive during the lessons, told Jan tales about the kittens, and eagerly worked on cutting and pasting a growing stack of valentines. Judging from the size of the stack, he had to be making one for every cowhand on the ranch.

As she left, B.J. accompanying her to the car, Jan spotted Clark. He was in the corral, inspecting a group of horses, lifting hoofs, patting flanks and examining teeth.

"There's Daddy. Are you going to say hello?" B.J. asked.

It was a question that had only one answer. She set her briefcase on the porch and started toward the corral. B.J. trotted ahead, giving his father a quick hug, before reversing directions. Rue Nell was calling him for lunch. At Clark's urging, Jan remained and walked with him toward the stables.

Clark leaned over Speckles' stall and fed the pony a handful of oats. He dusted the grain from his hands and turned toward her. "Are you still mad at me?"

"No." The answer was truthful. Her anger had evaporated. "But I do wish that you had let well enough alone."

"I'm afraid I'll never be able to let anything about you alone, Jan."

His words caused her mouth to go dry and her brain to short circuit. She stared up at him dumbly and felt a surge of relief when he finally rescued her from that awkward state by kissing her. His face and lips were cold from the February wind, yet warmed immediately in the heat of the embrace.

Neither heard the approaching footfall, only the clearing of a throat as Garrett exclaimed in a bitter voice. "So that's the way it is."

Caught unaware, the two separated as if jolted apart. They stared at Garrett, at his hands repeatedly clenching into fists and unclenching. "Why you no good—"

"Stay out of this, Garrett! You've thrown your weight around too much as it is."

Garrett charged toward Clark, one of his fists now raised.

"Grandpa! Don't hit Daddy!" B.J. was standing there beside his pony's stall, tears beginning to run down his cheeks. Before the rancher could respond, the child turned on his heel and dashed toward the house.

Both Clark and Garrett started after him, but Jan's voice stopped them in their tracks. "What are you stubborn fools going to do now? Follow him to the house and continue this stupid tug-of-war? I'm disgusted with the two of you! I don't care if I never see either of you again." With that, she pushed past them and ran toward her car. As much as she wanted to rush to B.J.'s side, Jan knew there was nothing she could do to rectify the situation. When she glanced back, both Clark and Garrett were standing where she'd left them.

What she had feared had come true. Giving in to her feelings for Clark had hurt both Garrett and B.J. Something she wouldn't have done for the world. But that kiss couldn't be undone, nor could the fact of Garrett's witnessing it. How could things have gotten so out of hand?

CHAPTER TWELVE

AS SHE drove toward town, Jan's level of distress continued to rise. That shouting match would never have happened if she'd backed away from Clark's kiss. It was all her fault. She could have kicked herself. Without doubt, she was jinxed in the love department. Yet her pulse still accelerated just thinking about Clark's cool lips, his warm breath on her face, the fluttering sensation in her chest.

If Garrett hadn't interrupted, no telling what might have developed. Jan would like to believe she had more sense than to opt for a roll in the hay with Clark Brennan, but at the moment, she had to admit that's exactly what could have happened. And what if B.J. had stumbled in earlier? That would have been even worse than Garrett's untimely entrance.

Her fretting continued so that when she reached the outskirts of Valentine, Jan knew she had to talk to Sally. By habit, she headed down Main Street toward the post office. Her aunt still would be there, completing last-minute details and straightening up after the prior week's rush.

Sally was alone when she arrived. "Hi, dear. Would you believe this?" She gestured toward the counters, clean and uncluttered. "I'm actually going to get out of here at closing time today. Are you fixing dinner?"

"Sure," Jan answered mechanically, food the farthest thing from her mind. "But first, can we talk?" She dropped onto the stool by the counter.

Sally sat down beside her and waited for Jan to begin. Long moments passed. "Something happened today, something dreadful," Jan began.

"And what was that?"

"It started when Clark kissed me."

Sally smiled. "I certainly can't imagine a kiss from *that* particular man being dreadful."

"Garrett walked in on us."

"So? Garrett knows all about the birds and the bees."

"Aunt Sally, you know how much I adore Garrett, how grateful I am to him. He's been as generous and supportive to me as you have, treated me like a member of his own family. And how have I repaid him? By betraying him. You should have seen how he looked—so disappointed...so shattered...." Tears formed in Jan's eyes.

"And you feel responsible?"

"I suppose I do. But there's more."

"Yes?" Sally prompted.

"Because of the kiss, Garrett and Clark got into a shouting match, a near fight, then B.J. came in."

"Oh, dear." Sally patted her arm. "What happened?"

"B.J. ran off crying and I told those other two 'boys' just what I thought of them for putting him in the middle."

"Good for you. Did they listen?"

"I don't know. I left...I probably should have stayed, tried to—"

"Nonsense. It was just as well you did leave. It's high time they worked out matters on their own."

"But what if they don't?"

"Quit worrying, honey. You're taking too much of this upon yourself. First off, that young one is more resilient than you think. Sure he's been hurting, but so has Garrett. Clark, too, I suspect. They're all in a healing process, licking their wounds. This blow-up was bound to happen. It was just a matter of time. So don't let it get to you."

Sally got up and gave Jan a hug.

Momentarily, the warmth of her aunt's embrace and the gentleness in her words soothed Jan. Again she reflected upon that remarkable something about Sally MacGuire approaching clairvoyance. Not your ordinary pie-in-the-sky prognosticator, but possessor of an uncommonly canny ability to assess situations and predict the outcomes. She was rarely wrong—if she said things were going to be okay, they usually were.

Months ago she'd assured Jan that her heartbreak over Glen would lighten with each passing day. Not such a difficult forecast, perhaps, but to Jan who pictured herself in mourning for the rest of her life, the notion seemed absurd. However, Sally had been right. Jan might never be able to fully purge her ex-husband from her thoughts, but the memories of him no longer seared her soul.

In this particular instance though, Jan suspected Sally of employing more heart than head and letting her personal preferences get in the way. As pragmatic as Sally might be, she was still the eternal optimist and favored platitudes about looking on the bright side. So Jan just returned Sally's hug and said goodbye, wishing that she could trust in her aunt's wisdom and positive feelings about the future.

Shortly after she arrived home, Clark pulled into the drive. Even though she had no inkling of what she could expect from this visit, Jan was glad he'd come. She met him at the door. "How's B.J.?"

"He's fine. Everyone's fine."

Jan looked at him skeptically. There was no way that acrimonious scene in the barn had been smoothed over in a matter of hours. "How could you possibly—"

"We talked, Garrett and I . . . then we went to B.J. and all three of us talked." Clark put his arm around her shoulder and guided her out to the garden room. "Everything's under control."

Jan scoffed. "That would have taken an act of God."

"Maybe that's what it was. As if finally seeing the light, Garrett and I realized you were right. There were only two avenues available to us—continuing to hurt B.J. or trying to get along. The first choice was, of course, unthinkable, so we had to figure out a way to tolerate one another for his sake."

"And how do you plan to accomplish that?"

"B.J.'s going to live with me—at the old Phillips' place and he'll make frequent visits to the Lazy M." Clark smiled. "It was amazingly easy to get Garrett to agree, Jan."

From everything Garrett had said to date, there was no way he would ever accept such an arrangement. "I can't think of a single thing that would make that happen. Unless you shoved a court order in his face or held a gun to his head."

Clark smiled. "Nothing so drastic. I simply told him we were getting married."

Married! Jan felt like screaming in frustration. *That* was how Clark had calmed Garrett—by claiming he and Jan were planning a wedding? "Of all the idiotic, ridiculous things to do!"

"The idea of you as B.J.'s stepmother is very appealing to Garrett. So much so that he isn't angry anymore," Clark responded.

"He may not be, but I am. How dare you use me to solve your problems with him! You've just gotten yourself out of one fix and into a worse one. I can only hope Garrett hasn't already called Sally... if so, well, she'll be so ecstatic the entire populace of Valentine probably knows, too. You get on that phone right this instant and tell him it was all a stupid mistake."

"I don't see any mistake. In my opinion, it's a wonderful idea. And you'll agree, too, as soon as you calm down and think it over."

"No. I don't intend to calm down until you—" The ringing telephone interrupted her.

It was Sally. Garrett *had* called her and she was positively bubbling. "See, I told you everything would work out. To think that you'll be living here in Valentine. It's like my prayers have been answered...."

The conversation lasted several minutes with Sally doing most of the talking. Jan's only opportunity to torpedo the marriage notion would have been to interrupt her aunt and coldly blurt it out. Something she hadn't the heart to do. Drat Clark anyway. He might as well have taken out an ad in the newspaper or painted his intentions on one of the billboards at the edge of town. By evening, her parents would probably be calling from Europe to offer congratulations. She hung up the receiver and slumped her shoulders. "Well, Mr. Fix It, you got us into this mess. Now it's your job to get us out."

"No problem. We'll just get married like I told Garrett. That's the simplest thing."

"Oh, right," she answered sarcastically.

"It would solve everything."

"Get real, Clark. Marriage doesn't solve problems—it creates them. You know that as well as I do."

"We wouldn't have that kind of marriage, Jan." He wrapped his arms around her.

She sighed loudly. Even facing the unflattering prospect that Clark might be using her, Jan felt a genuine excitement about the idea. In spite of everything, she loved Clark. *But then, you thought you loved Glen, too.*

"How can you be so annoyingly certain when I'm so confused?" She tried to pull away, but Clark wouldn't release her. "We're not what you'd call star players in the game of love," she grumbled.

"Maybe we learned a lot the first time around," he said. "Not stars, exactly, but experienced veterans."

"That's precisely what worries me. We're supposed to know all the pitfalls." She focused straight ahead, unable to keep her mind from drifting back to that other time, when she'd believed she was in love.

Clark's thumb making feathering strokes against her skin recaptured her full attention. "Maybe we were saving ourselves for the second round, Jan."

"There's not going to be a second round for me. I promised myself that." To even contemplate marrying him was preposterous. She attempted to ignore the sensations his touch was creating, making it hard for her to concentrate. "I don't want to talk about this anymore."

"What you need is time to get used to the idea. I've been thinking about it so much—every minute since those days we were snowed in.... I guess I'd been presuming you'd been doing the same thing. Garrett's dance is Saturday. Maybe you could give me an answer then?"

Jan had completely forgotten about the dance. Despite all the turmoil Garrett was going through, he'd never broached the subject of canceling. Sally's influence at work, no doubt. But then, the annual event was a cherished tradition in Valentine. "Okay, I'll try." She had no confidence that she'd feel any different by Saturday, but at least she'd have Clark off her case for a while.

"Just to show you my heart's in the right place, I'm going to give you time alone to weigh your decision," he added. "Especially since I know you can't think straight when I'm around."

"That's not true," she protested. "I—"

"Don't bother denying it. Everyone but you knows you're crazy about me." He tipped her chin and quickly kissed her. "Actually I'll be gone anyway. I need to make a trip to New York to meet with my publisher. I won't be back until the weekend. So will you promise to give me an answer at the dance?"

Jan nodded. Heaven only knew what that answer would be, but she'd make up her mind by then, even if she had to flip a coin. There had been too much confusion in everyone's lives already without her adding to the strain.

Once Clark was gone, her internal debate began in earnest. Was the proposal merely his way of nailing down custody of B.J.? Jan knew that was a distinct possibility, even a probability. And loving B.J. as much as she did, she could imagine doing the same thing if the shoe were on the other foot. The main question was whether a marriage between her and Clark stood a chance of succeeding.

She'd known Clark such a short period. Not that time guaranteed success. She and Glen hadn't really known one another, despite their many years of courtship. But if a marriage founded on a long-term relationship could flounder so badly, was there any hope for an impetuous, spur-of-the-moment one? What would it take for her to feel confident about Clark?

Trying to explain her indecision to Sally was difficult, but her aunt was as supportive as ever, even though Jan suspected she was hoping for a Valentine's Day miracle, a romantic miracle.

The big day dawned with no miracle and no decision. The flowers Clark had sent were lovely, Jan's favorite, no less—a delicate nosegay of violets delivered all the way from Temple. But they didn't help her make up her mind. Nor did a second gift—this time candy in a big heart-shaped box. Yet when Clark telephoned, the sound of his voice almost made her want to say "yes."

"Did the flowers arrive?"

"Yes, the candy, too. Am I to consider them a bribe?" She found herself unable to keep the soft, teasing tone from her voice.

"If it works, yes." After a moment of her silence, Clark added, "Which it obviously didn't. Oh, well, you can't fault a guy for trying. I miss you, Jan. While we've been apart, I've done a lot of thinking. It dawned on me that we haven't so much as had one *real* date—unless you count that lunch in Temple. The flowers and candy are just a start on making that up to you."

"It's not important."

"It is to me. I don't want you to assume all this is because of B.J."

But is it? Jan still couldn't dismiss the notion. "Clark, I need to go. I promised to relieve Sally for an hour while she carries some cards and cookies to the nursing home. We'll talk tonight." She hung up the receiver, the fears that it was *all because of B.J.* stronger than ever.

Jan nervously smoothed the skirt of her red dress as she and Sally waited for Garrett to open the door and welcome them to the dance. Everyone in Valentine and from neighboring towns had been invited, so there would be several hundred guests on the scene once the party got in full swing. A late arrival would have been preferable to Jan so she could get lost in the crowd. But Sally Mac, as punctual as a time clock, had insisted they arrive on the dot, making them the first ones there.

"Hello, Garrett," Jan said warily. She hadn't seen him since the confrontation in the barn. Every time she came for lessons, he was gone into town or out with the cattle. Jan had decided he was purposely keeping out of her way.

"Hello, Jan." His face was without expression, then it broke into a sheepish smile as he pulled her into one of his big bear hugs. "I'm sorry about what happened Monday."

"It's over," she said, her voice muffled by the hug. "I'm sorry, too, I—"

"Then let's just forget it. Clark's told me about your plans and I'll have to admit I'm pleased as punch."

Garrett sounded like he'd been sampling the punch—the alcoholic one concocted of a local recipe of rum, brandy and one-hundred-proof bourbon—and was acting as if a decision had already been made. Apparently, neither Clark nor Sally had told him the whole story. By the end of the evening, though, he'd know. She'd arrived undecided but suddenly the realization had come to her that there was only one answer. A marriage between them had no chance of succeeding. She'd tell Clark as soon as the opportunity presented itself.

Her resolve was momentarily tested when Clark entered, walking right over and boldly kissing her in front of Garrett, Sally and B.J. Jan gently pulled away, trying to appear blasé and hide her embarrassment at the same time. Fortunately the sound of approaching horns and voices rescued her. Cars and pickups were filling the drive, the ranch hands directing them with flashlights toward the barn. "It's time to get on down there," Garrett told them. "I hear the music starting."

All evening Jan was frustrated by Clark's successful ploys to avoid any serious discussions. It was almost as though he sensed what she wanted to say and was determined she would not have an opportunity to do so. Considering they'd danced almost every number—from a waltz to a two-step to the cotton-eyed joe—it was a remarkable accomplishment. But then, again, there was no privacy. One of the ranch hands would cut in, or the band was too loud, or Clark would stonewall her forays into the matter by changing the subject. *Darn you, Clark*

Brennan, she thought, wanting to have this over and done with.

Later in the evening, when the first guests were saying their goodbyes, Clark pulled her over to Garrett, B.J. and Sally. "I think we'll get out of here, if you don't mind. There are a lot of things we need to discuss."

Garrett clapped him on the shoulder as if the two were best buddies who had never exchanged a cross word in their lives. Sally kissed them both. B.J. gave enthusiastic hugs. They were just walking away, when the child called her back. "Are you going to be my new mother?" he whispered in her ear.

Jan couldn't bring herself to answer. She couldn't lie to the boy but the truth seemed unbelievably cruel, both to B.J. and to herself. "We'll talk about it tomorrow, okay?"

His snaggle-toothed, seven-year-old smile showed that for him, everything was perfect.

"Why did you tell B.J. we were getting married?" Jan started in on Clark the moment he settled himself behind the steering wheel of his new truck.

"I didn't, Garrett did."

"So why didn't you level with Garrett instead of letting him spread this cock-and-bull story around?"

"Sounds like you've made up your mind." Clark's voice was surprisingly calm as he pulled out of the drive and shifted into first gear. Soon they were on the highway headed toward his ranch.

"Take me home!"

He kept driving. "Sally Mac will be returning before long. We need to be alone. You haven't given me your reply. I want to hear the words from your own lips."

"I can't marry you. It just won't work. Surely you can see that."

"No. What I see is you trying to avoid a second round of calamity. If I could, I'd promise to protect you from that, unfortunately I can't. All I can do is everything in my power to make you happy, but I can't pretend there won't be bumps along the way. Nobody can control fate. Life's not that way, Jan. Misery and misfortune are always in the wings—for anyone, anytime. I know that from all the heartache I saw in the war zones."

"Then why do you want to take a chance on creating more?"

"Because I don't look at things the way you do," he said. "You may think there's safety in wrapping yourself in a cocoon. But I see that as an empty existence. My experiences made me realize that you have to grab happiness while you can." He took her hand. "And you meant happiness to me right from the start." He released her hand a moment to shift gears as he turned into the long drive to his house. Jan felt bereft at the break in contact.

"I happen to think being your husband would be about the greatest thing that could possibly happen to me. Along with having B.J., of course. When I daydream about the years ahead I see only good times."

"That's wishful thinking," she argued, but even as she said the words, Jan's conviction was faltering. She thought about how life could be. Not the big-city hassles with a fast-track career taking precedence over happiness, but low-key, chore-filled days at Clark's ranch, with him and B.J., and maybe later, a baby.

Her thoughts must have been evident from her expression because Clark stopped the truck halfway down the drive and cut the engine. He got out, coming around to open her door and help her outside. Even though it was quite late, the February evening was mild. A sliver of new moon arced in the sky and millions of stars dotted the heavens. Clark pulled her into his embrace.

"I was rather skeptical of that heart-shaped sign that welcomes visitors to Valentine," he said. "And all that Chamber of Commerce ballyhoo about the lovers' holiday seemed to me commercial overkill...then I met you. I'm beginning to wonder whether those stars we see are cupids pointing their arrows. I know I've been hit—hard. I love you, Jan."

Dare she believe? Were the moon and stars casting some sort of spell on her...she certainly felt that the night was magical. She looked into Clark's glittering eyes and in them found the courage to trust. She realized now what she had to say. "I love you, too."

"Then you'll marry me, stay here in Valentine with me?"

She nodded.

"I promise a Valentine's Day every day for the rest of our lives."

"I think a month of it will be quite enough," she teased.

Clark smiled. "Whatever you say. But just in case you change your mind...." He reached into his pocket and pulled out a ring box. "I've been carrying this darned thing around for days waiting for this moment." He opened the box to reveal a heart-shaped diamond. "I figured this is the only appropriate ring for this crazy day and this crazy place."

"It's perfect," Jan said, as he slipped it onto her finger. "I love it. Almost as much as I love you."

"Then your doubts are gone and you'll be my wife?"

There must be some additive in the town's drinking water, Jan thought wryly. Some secret potion that affected even the most disinclined and made them susceptible to love. She no longer cared though. "Yes, oh, yes," she answered, her lips meeting his in a kiss. Just before she closed her eyes, a shooting star crossed the sky and Jan knew for sure that Sally's miracle had come true—Cupid had found his mark.